BOOT CAMP

BOOT CAMP

TODD STRASSER

Simon Pulse
New York London Toronto Sydney

SIMON PULSE
An imprint of Simon & Schuster Children's Publishing Division
1230 Avenue of the Americas, New York, NY 10020
Copyright © 2007 by Todd Strasser
All rights reserved, including the right of reproduction
in whole or in part in any form.
SIMON PULSE and colophon are registered trademarks
of Simon & Schuster, Inc.
Also available in a Simon & Schuster Books for Young Readers
hardcover edition.
Designed by Einav Aviram
The text of this book was set in Aldus LT Std.
Manufactured in the United States of America
First Simon Pulse edition July 2008
8 10 9
The Library of Congress has cataloged the hardcover edition as follows:
Strasser, Todd.
Boot camp / Todd Strasser—1st ed.
p. cm.
Summary: After ignoring several warnings to stop dating his teacher,
Garrett is sent to Lake Harmony, a boot camp that uses unorthodox
and brutal methods to train students to obey their parents.
ISBN-13: 978-1-4169-0848-7 (hc)
ISBN-10: 1-4169-0848-X (hc)
[1. Juvenile delinquency—Fiction. 2. Interpersonal relationships—Fiction.
3. Family problems—Fiction.] I. Title.
PZ7.S899Boo 2007
[Fic]—dc22
2006013634
ISBN-13: 978-1-4169-5942-7 (pbk)
ISBN-10: 1-4169-5942-4 (pbk)

To Laura,
with love
and
thanks

"You don't get out by giving them what you *think* they want. You don't get out until you *are* what they want."

—Pauly

ONE

"Your parents sent you to Lake Harmony because they love you."

"Excuse me. My hands are numb."

"So?" replies the man driving the car. His name is Harry.

"Maybe you could loosen the handcuffs?" I ask.

"Sorry, blue blood."

"If you're sorry, then why don't you help me?"

"No can do." Harry wears a cowboy hat and speaks with a western accent. From my seat in the back of the dark car I can only see the silhouette of his shoulders and thick neck beneath the wide-brimmed hat. My hands, locked behind me for the past two hours, have gone numb. I feel nothing but tingling from my wrists down.

"Would you at least tell me where you're taking me?" I ask.

Harry doesn't answer. The car bounces and lurches through the dark. Except for the short stretch of dusty, reddish dirt road illuminated by the headlights, it is as black as blindness outside. Rocks kicked up by the tires clank against the car's underside. The air-conditioning murmurs. Now and then sudsy spray splashes against the windshield, and the wipers wash away dust and splattered bug carcasses.

With my hands joined by the handcuffs in the small of my back, there is no way to get comfortable, no way to relieve the pressure that has cut off the circulation.

"When my parents hired you, did they know that physical abuse was part of the deal?" I ask.

From the movement of his head, I sense that Harry is looking at me in the rearview mirror, but his eyes are hidden in the shadow from the rim of his hat. "That was some spread we picked you up from, blue blood. What's your father's business that he can afford a place like that?"

Harry's been calling me blue blood ever since he and the woman riding shotgun took me against my will from my parents' house, drove me to the airport, and flew me to upstate New York.

"You really want to know what my father does? How about loosening these handcuffs and I'll tell you."

"Nice try, partner." Harry chuckles. The woman

sitting beside him turns to look over the seat at me. Her name is Rebecca, and she is younger than Harry. In the eight hours since they grabbed me, I've learned that Rebecca is new to the business of kidnapping for hire (Harry prefers you call him a "transporter"). She has a pretty face and streaked blond hair with dark roots. But there is a hardness around her eyes and mouth that makes me think of someone older.

"Can you feel anything at all?" she asks.

"No. I'm worried I'll have permanent nerve damage or something."

In the dark car, she turns to Harry. "Couldn't you loosen them just a little?"

"Fat chance," Harry chuckles. "Come on, sugarplum, you've been there. You know how it works. First rule is, don't believe a word these kids say. You loosen those cuffs, next he'll say he needs to relieve himself by the side of the road. Now how's he gonna do that with his hands cuffed behind him, right? So he swears on his mother's grave if you undo them he won't run. Next thing you know, you're chasing him through the woods cussing yourself for being such a fool."

Once again Rebecca glances over the seat at me. Even in the shadows I can sense her uncertainty.

"What does he mean, 'you've been there'?" I ask.

"I've been where you're going," she answers.

"Why?" I ask.

Before Rebecca can answer, Harry snaps, "That's none of your business, blue blood. I've heard enough out of you. Now shut it."

"One last thing," I tell him. "I really do have to go.

You've been with me for the last eight hours, so you know I'm telling the truth. And I give you my word that I won't run."

"Ha! Now *that* is what we call manipulation," Harry says with just a hint of annoyance. "See how the moment he acts agreeable it makes you feel sympathetic toward him? Like he can't be such a bad kid, right? Giving you his word and all. Well, sugarplum, that's the first step toward him trying to get you on his side."

Rebecca gives him an astonished look, as if that is precisely what she's feeling.

"Never forget, these kids have had years of experience lying, manipulating, doing whatever it takes to get what they want," Harry counsels her. "That's why their parents hired us. That's why they're paying four grand a month to send him where he's going."

Rebecca swivels her head and faces stiffly forward. I wonder if she feels angry or humiliated now that Harry has demonstrated how easy it is to fall under the spell of my "evil" ways.

In silence we bump down the narrow dirt road. I yawn and wish I could stretch. It was after midnight when we landed at the airport in Utica. Now it must be close to three A.M.

"How much longer?" I ask.

Neither Harry nor Rebecca answers. Rocks bang against the undercarriage of the car. The potholes are getting bigger, and we toss and heave like a boat on rough seas.

"So I guess when I said I really did have to go to the bathroom, you didn't believe me."

My words are met with silence.

"Or maybe you'll say, 'Go right ahead, it's not your car, why should you care?'"

Harry reaches up and adjusts the rearview mirror. This time our eyes meet. "I told you to shut it, blue blood." His voice drops ominously with the implicit threat *or else*. After a few more minutes he veers onto another dirt road. In the distance, through the dusty windshield, I can see dim lights, which gradually grow brighter. We stop before a tall chain-link fence topped with loops of razor wire. A man steps out of a small white booth and shines a flashlight into the car. Rebecca shields her eyes from the glare. I have to turn my face. The man seems to recognize Harry. He unlocks the gate and we drive through, past a dark basketball court and a bare flagpole, and pull into a gravel parking lot.

"Here we are." Harry jumps out of the car with unexpected energy after the long ride. He comes around to my door and pulls me out with a firm grip. After sitting in that awkward position for so long, my legs and back are stiff, and I straighten up unsteadily. But I also feel a brief wave of relief, as standing temporarily takes the excruciating pressure off my bladder, which has felt near bursting for at least half an hour. I shake out my legs and glance around.

"Trust me, blue blood, don't be thinking about running," Harry warns. "Even if you got through the fence, there's nothing but forest out there. You're so far away from civilization, you'll starve before you see another human being."

The air is cool and smells like pine. The chatter of

crickets is almost as loud as traffic on a city street. In the dark I can make out four or five buildings, none more than two stories tall.

Then the crickets go silent.

And I hear screaming.

TWO

"You must accept the fact that you deserved to be sent to Lake Harmony."

I'm allowed to use the bathroom. Then I'm put in a small, windowless room with a military-style, metal-framed bed. Two stern-looking men wearing matching black polo shirts and khaki slacks sit in chairs by the door. One is tall with dark skin, a muscular build, and an athlete's natural grace. The other is short, bulky, and troll-like, with dark stubble around his jaw and a square head that disappears into his shoulders with almost no sign of a neck. Together they remind me of the seated stone giants who guard the tomb of Ramses.

"You guys here to make sure I don't escape?" I ask as I sit down on the bare mattress.

"Stand up and shut up," the troll orders.

I'm tired—it must be four A.M. by now—and would prefer to lie down and sleep, but something tells me to obey, so I stand. The men in the chairs watch me. The tall one yawns. This must be boring as hell for them. It sure is for me.

"How long do I have to stand here?" I ask after a while.

"Shut up," the troll grunts. Even his tone sounds bored. There's no vehemence in the words.

So I stand, and stand, and stand. An hour passes, then another. I shift my weight from one foot to the other, arch my back, and wonder, How much longer is this going to last?

Sitting in the chair, the tall, dark-skinned one starts to close his eyes. His head begins to droop. The troll notices and nudges him with his elbow. The tall one jerks his head up with a start, then yawns.

Outside, a bird chirps, and even in this windowless room I sense that the sky has gone from black to gray. I yawn and stretch and more than anything want to lie down and sleep, but both men keep a steady eye on me, and I know what the answer will be if I ask.

How much longer? While I don't know the answer to that particular question, I have a feeling I do know the answer to another: *Why am I here?* Because my parents are trying to scare me into "behaving." I'll admit that this time I'm impressed by the lengths to which they've gone. Arranging for me to be taken against my will is pretty extreme. Back in the city Sabrina will be waking up soon. She'll wait for me to call. But that call won't come, and she won't know why, and she won't be able to find out unless she calls my parents, who have consistently refused to meet or speak to her. It's hard to imagine they will now.

From outside come the sounds of early-morning stirring. The slam of a car door. Footsteps in the hallway. The door opens. A thin man with slicked-back black hair and a thin black mustache enters carrying a brown paper shopping bag. He's wearing a white polo shirt and khaki slacks, and he stares at me with puffy, reddened eyes. His nose twitches every time he sniffs.

"Strip," he orders.

The word is so unexpected that I assume I heard him incorrectly. "Sorry?"

"You heard me," he barks.

Yes, I heard him, but . . . The men in the chairs sit up, more alert.

"Who are you?" I ask.

The thin man narrows his swollen eyes. "That's the last time you will speak unless spoken to. You will remain silent and do what you're told when you're told." He checks his watch. "You have exactly twenty seconds to get out of those clothes, or you'll stand here until this time tomorrow when we'll try again."

I want to tell him to go to hell, but I have a feeling that's exactly what he expects. I may not know where I am, but I do know these three men have the advantage. This may be new to me, but it isn't to them. They've been through this a hundred, maybe even a thousand, times before.

I kick off my shoes, then start to unbutton my shirt. The thin man glances at his watch impatiently, but whether from fatigue or disbelief or anger I can't get my fingers to work more quickly.

"Faster!" the thin man barks.

Every fiber in my body yearns to refuse. But doing so will only delay what I really need to accomplish, which is to get out of here and back to Sabrina. So I finish unbuttoning my shirt and yank it off, then open my belt buckle and start to pull down my pants. The men in the chairs glance at each other and the tall one raises his eyebrow, as if they're surprised I've cooperated so quickly.

Meanwhile the thin man sniffs and consults his watch. I push my pants down over my ankles and step out of them. The thin man's eyes dart at my feet, then back to his watch, so I quickly strip off my socks. Now I'm only in my boxers.

He nods. "Those too."

Anger boils up inside me and I want to shout, *Why? Who the hell do you think you are?* But I already know the answer. I've read about places like this, and I've seen the TV specials. I had hours in the airport and on the plane and in the car to figure it out. I'm in a boot camp, and its purpose is to break me down and "train" me, like a cowboy breaks a bronco or a dog is taught in obedience school.

The thin man glances at his watch again. "See you tomorrow." He turns toward the door.

"Wait." I push the boxer shorts down, then step out of them.

The thin man stops. I'm standing naked and defenseless, and these three men are staring at me. It's not cold in the room, but shivers race over my skin like chilling winds.

"Turn around and bend over."

Just when you thought it couldn't get any worse . . .

The troll smiles. He's enjoying this. Meanwhile, my legs won't move.

"You want to spend the next twenty-four hours standing in that spot?" the thin man asks.

I turn and bend. Strangely, this isn't as difficult as I might have thought. Now that they've made me strip, what difference does it make?

"Spread 'em."

Do it, I tell myself. For Sabrina. *The sooner I'm out of here, the sooner we'll be together again.*

When he's done searching, the thin man puts my clothes in the paper bag. In their place he leaves a green polo shirt, blue jeans, and green flip-flops. He departs while I'm putting on my new uniform. Once dressed, I assume the two men are going to take me somewhere else. But they remain seated.

"Try to get some sleep," the tall one says.

"I have to stay here?" I ask.

"No talking!" the troll barks.

I'm not about to argue with a chance to rest, so I lie on my back on the bare mattress, stare at the lightbulb hanging from the ceiling, and wonder how long my parents had been planning this.

THREE

"You will not stand, sit, or talk without permission."

A hand shakes my shoulder. "Wake up."

I open my eyes. The ceiling light is still on. A man in a black polo shirt whom I haven't seen before hovers over me.

"Time to go," he says.

I don't know what time it is, only that heavy tentacles of sleep are pulling my head back down to the pillow. I close my eyes but instantly feel the hand on my shoulder again, rougher this time. "Get up."

Groggily I try to bat the hand away, but feel him grab my wrist and expertly twist. The next thing I know, I'm rolled onto my side on the bed. His grip tightens and pain shoots through my shoulder, as if he's trying to pry my arm out of joint.

I croak through clenched teeth. "Okay, okay."

He backs off slightly and the pain eases. In a practiced tone he recites: "Your parents have signed and notarized a consent form allowing Lake Harmony to use restraint whenever necessary. The type and degree of restraint administered shall be at the discretion of the staff. Lake Harmony and its employees will not be held liable for any injury sustained by you during the administration of restraint as it is understood that such injury is the result of willful disobedience on your part. Now get up."

In my father's world they call this the CYA ("cover your a**") statement. As I slowly get up from the bed, the man keeps my arm behind my back. Part of me wants to resist, but another part of me knows there is no move I can make that he has not seen before.

"If I let go of your arm, will you do what you're told?" he asks.

"Yes."

"Yes, what?"

"Yes . . . sir?"

He lets go and opens the door. "You first."

I step out into a hallway and then through a metal door to the outside. The day is bright and the sky blue, the early morning air moist and fragrant. Some of the trees are covered with reddish buds and the beginnings of small bright-green leaves. A few have small white or pink flowers. We walk across a grassy yard. Fifty yards away, a woman wearing a white polo shirt marches a single-file line of girls between buildings. The girls are dressed in red polo shirts, jeans, and flip-flops. They march with silent military precision, roughly three feet apart, eyes forward.

We go into an old brick building with round, castlelike turrets. Inside is a small lobby with two couches and a table with some flowers, magazines, and brochures about Lake Harmony, "a highly structured boarding school specializing in intensive behavior modification." On the walls are framed "class pictures": smiling young people in rows, just like you might find in a small private school. At the far end of the room is a dark wooden door. The white letters on the rectangular black plaque read: DIRECTOR.

"Go on," the black polo shirt orders.

I cross the lobby to the door, then stop and look back at him.

"Knock."

I do as I'm told, and a gruff voice from inside says, "Come in."

I push open the door. A stocky man sits at a desk, staring down at some papers through thin half-glasses, forehead wrinkled as if the act of reading takes intense concentration. His gray hair is cut short, and his nose is crooked, probably broken a long time ago. A small gold hoop pierces one earlobe. The rolled-up sleeves of his shirt reveal muscular forearms, and his hands are rough and faintly scarred, his fingers stubby and thick. He looks like someone who is used to working with those hands rather than sitting at a desk.

I wait while he reads. My head has begun to hurt.

Craving coffee, I glance around the office, hoping there might be a pot brewing in some corner, but there isn't. Instead there are dark-green file cabinets, some wooden chairs, a megaphone, and a wall map of the United States with different colored pins stuck into it.

Finally, he stacks the papers and places them in a folder. Looking at me for the first time, he holds the folder with both hands and wags it. "Kid hit his mother so hard, he broke her jaw." He sighs as he says this. As if he's never heard of such a thing before. "Tell me, Garrett, you ever hit your mother?"

"No."

"No, *sir*," he corrects, and gestures to a chair on the other side of the desk. "Sit down."

I sit. His eyes are a washed-out gray, the color of hazy rain clouds. He makes a tent with his stubby fingers. "Welcome to Lake Harmony, Garrett. I'm Mr. Z, and I am the director of this facility. I assume by now you've figured out why you're here. Your parents are paying a substantial amount of money because they are seriously concerned about your welfare. They want you to return home as soon as possible. How long you stay is up to you. I've seen students graduate after six months. Others have taken three years or longer. The choice is yours."

He opens a desk drawer, takes out a thick, stapled document, and hands it to me. "This is your bible. Read it carefully. Study it. When you feel you've learned it completely, you may request a test. Once you have passed the test, you will be ready to join your fellow students."

He pauses and gazes steadily into my eyes. "Any questions?"

"Can I get a cup of coffee . . . uh, sir?" I ask.

"You'll be forgoing all caffeinated drinks during your stay here," Mr. Z informs me. Hearing those words hurts almost as much as my headache. "Any other questions?"

"Sir, is it possible that someone could be sent here for the wrong reason?" I ask.

Those gray eyes don't waver. Once again I have the feeling that this is a question he's heard a thousand times before. Mr. Z shakes his head. "Children are sent here by their parents, Garrett."

"And . . . parents are always right, sir?"

"That is the principle under which we operate. At least until a child reaches the age of emancipation," Mr. Z replies.

"Eighteen?"

"Sorry?" he snaps.

"Eighteen . . . sir?"

"In most states."

Another silence. I glance at the wall map. The densest collections of pins are near the large metropolitan areas on both coasts. Mr. Z knows what I'm looking at, but he makes no effort to explain its meaning. Instead, he asks, "Any other questions?"

"No . . . sir."

"Very good. You can go."

Back outside, the man in the black polo shirt takes me to yet another building. This one has classrooms. Inside, students sit at carrels working silently at computers. The walls of the carrels prevent them from seeing the other students. Men and women in black or white polo shirts sit at the backs of the rooms and watch.

I am taken to an empty classroom and shown to a carrel. "Study it," the black shirt orders, nodding at the "bible" Mr. Z gave me. The introduction begins like this:

> You are now a member of the Lake Harmony community. You will be released when you are judged to be respectful, polite, and obedient enough to return to your family. During your stay here you will have no communication with the outside world, except for letters to your parents. After six months your parents may visit you for a day if they choose.

Despite having had only a few hours' sleep, not to mention the thumping caffeine headache, I manage to quickly read through the sixty-one-page document. It lists the rules: no talking, no touching, no disrespectful looks, etc. It describes the six levels one must rise through in order to be considered a candidate for "graduation." It explains the system of points one must earn to climb from one level to the next.

After about forty minutes I raise my hand.

"Bathroom?" the black shirt asks.

"I'm ready for the test, sir."

Black shirt frowns. "In less than an hour? No way. No one's ready that fast. Read it again."

I skim the bible again, then glance up. Black shirt doesn't look happy. "You're wasting my time," he mumbles, placing some photocopied sheets on my desk. The sheets have been copied so many times, the black letters have blurred and run together. There are fifteen questions, with room for one- or two-sentence answers.

Why have you been sent to Lake Harmony?
What does manipulation mean?
What must you do to graduate?

It takes about twenty minutes to complete the test.

Black shirt gazes doubtfully when I motion that I'm finished, as if not only is it impossible to learn the whole bible as fast as I claim, but even more impossible to complete the test. The frown on his face only deepens when he reads my answers, pausing now and then to refer back to the bible to make sure they are correct.

He finishes marking the test and pauses, drumming his fingertips rhythmically against the table. He checks his watch, looks down at the test again, then goes to a phone on the wall and makes a call. After a while there's a knock, and another black shirt sticks his head into the room. The two black shirts whisper, then come to a decision.

With one in front of me and the other behind, I'm escorted back to the windowless room with the metal bed. The black shirts sit in the chairs, while I remain standing, waiting for the next order. *My parents have signed all the necessary legal documents . . .*

I'm here for a minimum of six months . . .

"Take a nap," one black shirt tells me. "You must be tired."

"Not really." I should be tired, but I'm too wound up. And my head hurts too much.

"What?"

"Not really . . . sir."

"Then sit down and shut up."

This can't be real . . .

My parents say I began sounding out words in picture books around the age of two and a half. At four I scored off the charts on the Chester Scale, the entrance exam for the city's top private kindergartens. At age six I was figuring out square roots and adding radicals. For the first seven years of my life all I heard was how brilliant I was. Then, at the age of eight, I forged a letter from my mother excusing me from gym because of severe asthma. Sports were dumb, and I wasn't good at them. I even bought an inhaler at a drugstore and whipped it out whenever anything athletic was mentioned. The ruse lasted for nearly six months, until my second-grade teacher mentioned at a parent-teacher conference how badly she felt that I had to skip so many physical activities. From then on I was no longer brilliant. I was now too smart for my own good.

FOUR

"You will obey all orders immediately and without hesitation."

"Hey, big guy."

It's my second morning. I've been here for roughly thirty hours, and it's been one nonstop caffeine headache. I'm sitting at the end of a long table with my new "family." Our family name is Dignity, and we are 20 males wearing identical forest-green polo shirts and blue jeans, our hair and fingernails closely clipped (long nails are considered a weapon).

Our name may be Dignity, but from the looks of these guys it might as well be Losers. Maybe it's the headache, but I swear I've never seen a sketchier bunch of rejects. If it's too fat or too skinny, if it slouches or has bad zits or a permanently sour expression on its face, it's here. No one's allowed to speak to me, and frankly I'm more than okay with that. The less I have to do with this bunch, the better.

At other "family" tables, females wear jeans and red polo shirts. Lower-level males have had their hair shorn close to their skulls. The hair of lower-level females has been cut short. Only upper-level residents can grow their hair longer if they choose. Family "fathers" and "mothers" wear white polo shirts and khaki slacks. They patrol the tables, assisted by "chaperones" in black polo shirts and khakis.

Breakfast this morning consists of watery, lukewarm scrambled eggs, cold, soggy toast, and a powdered orange drink that makes Tang seem like champagne. The only eating implements allowed are white plastic spoons. Through speakers hanging from the ceiling a taped lecture thunders: *"Good posture is important because it helps your body function at top speed. It promotes movement efficiency and endurance and contributes to an overall feeling of wellness."*

The tape is so loud, it's painful. I suspect it has two purposes. The obvious one is to cajole residents to focus on self-improvement. The less obvious purpose is to make it difficult for us to communicate with each other. But the ridiculously loud volume also has the opposite effect, allowing students to communicate without being noticed.

"Hey you, big guy."

The whispers come during the brief moments in

the tape when the reader pauses to catch his breath. The kid doing the whispering is sitting at the middle of our table. He's got short reddish hair and freckles that dot his face like a smallpox victim. His lips curl into a nasty smirk that reveals small, yellow, reptilian teeth, and his eyelids are pale pink like an albino's. Seated around him is his posse, guys who stare fiercely at me as if they mean to project a big attitude. But it's the red-haired kid who's making trouble.

"What's wrong, big guy, afraid to talk?"

He knows that I'm not allowed to speak without permission.

"Big guy, or big chicken?"

I was always big for my age. Now I'm just big, period. Six feet four, 230 pounds, and broad-shouldered, even if I am the opposite of athletic. It's genetics—just the way I was born. You would assume it's a bonus to be tall, and in some ways I guess you'd be right. But you'd also be surprised. Everyone assumes I'm a great basketball player, which I'm not. At least once a day I manage to bang my head in a low doorway. And sometimes I'm a target for smaller guys with Napoleon complexes—like this red-haired jerk—who think they have something to prove.

"Bawk, bawk, bawk." The freckled kid makes chicken sounds. The guys around him grin.

Since I'm the new kid, my "father" is keeping an extra sharp eye on me. His name is Joe, and he is the thin, black-haired man who ordered me to strip in the windowless room when I first arrived. Joe's eyes are puffy and red from spring allergies, and his nose twitches constantly. He seems convinced that we are always up to no good. Already this morning I had to do twenty push-ups (the last ten on my knees) for not tucking in my shirt properly, while Joe screamed that I was a lazy, good-for-nothing slob with low self-esteem and no self-respect. I wanted to ask why he thought that, since he didn't know me at all. Of course, being a Level One, I couldn't say anything.

The red-haired kid goes quiet when Joe cruises slowly past our table. Joe's body language says he thinks he may have heard something. I take another spoonful of cold scrambled eggs and stare straight ahead, chewing. According to the rules I must eat at least half of every meal. If I don't, whatever is left over will be served to me again at the next meal. No sooner does Joe pass than a small glob of eggs hits me on the side of the nose. Wiping it off, I slowly turn my gaze toward the red-haired kid, who bares his lizard teeth for an instant.

"What was that, Garrett Durrell?" Suddenly Joe is standing over me with his hands planted firmly on his hips. His voice is loud enough for the entire food hall to hear.

"Sorry?" I answer.

"Sorry, what?" His twitching nose reminds me of a rabbit.

"Uh . . . sorry . . . sir."

"What are you so sorry about?" Joe's voice becomes shrill, like Hitler's when he was rallying the Nazis. I try not to stare at his nose. It takes concentration not to laugh.

"I . . . er . . . don't know . . . sir."

Joe's face tightens like a fist. "You disrespecting me, punk? You don't know what?"

The food hall has gone still. Not a tap of a spoon or a slurp of juice. I keep my eyes aimed down at the table, but I know they're all watching me.

"I don't know, sir."

"You don't know *what*?"

Maybe it's the omnipresent headache, but I've lost track of what this is about. I stare down at the table and don't answer.

"Stand up!" Joe shouts.

I do as I'm told. My tired legs tremble and my sore knees ache when I put weight on them. Earlier this morning we had to run five miles in military-style leather boots through woods, across muddy streams, and up and down hills. We were not allowed to stop or walk. Those who grew too tired to run were forced to crawl on their hands and knees until they could run again. Standing now in the food hall, I glance out of the corner of my eye at a family of females at the next table. I know they're watching, but when I look, they avert their eyes. Except for one who sits apart from the others, her black hair pulled to the side and her blue eyes clear and unwavering. A square, handwritten cardboard sign hangs around her neck:

TWO YEARS AND STILL PULLING THE SAME CRAP.

Her eyes meet mine with a steady, knowing gaze.

"Stand straight!" Joe shouts.

I straighten up and look down into Joe's face. Our

eyes meet. His are small, beady, and hard. His face is red with fury, and his forehead is lined. I can't understand what he's so angry about.

"What's that look?" he demands sharply.

"Sorry, sir?"

"You disrespecting me, Garrett?"

"No, sir."

Joe leans closer, his nose twitching rapidly. "You think you're smart, don't you?"

"No, sir."

"The hell you don't. Memorizing the whole bible in forty minutes."

Murmurs break out at the tables around us, only to be extinguished by harsh stares from "mothers" and "fathers."

"You got some kind of photographic memory? Naw, you're too stupid-looking." Joe grins as if he finds this amusing. "You just got lucky on the test, right?"

"Uh, yes, sir."

"Yes, sir, no, sir, yes, sir, no, sir. You think you can hide behind that 'sir' crap like it's some kind of protective shield? Forget it, punk. Anyone can see what's really going on. You think we're stupid, right? Well, that crap doesn't cut it here, understand?"

"Yes, sir." *Crap*, it appears, is a catchword for all undesirable behavior at Lake Harmony.

"Yeah, you . . . ah-choo!" Joe suddenly sneezes.

"Bless you, sir."

Joe whips out a disgusting, yellowed handkerchief and blows his nose. "Damn allergies." With watery, red-rimmed eyes he gives me a menacing look. "Did you say 'bless you'? What are you, my priest?"

I don't realize that he actually wants me to answer.

"Answer me, punk."

"No, sir, I'm not your priest."

"Is that the way people talk where you come from? Please, and thank you, and bless you?"

"Yes, sir."

"Everyone's all nice and civilized?"

"Only on the surface, sir."

My "father" scowls slightly, as if not certain what to make of this answer. "What does that mean?"

"It means that where I come from people pretend to act nice and civilized, sir. But they'll stab you in the back just the same."

Joe's eyebrows dip slightly. "So tell me something, Garrett Durrell—how in the world did you wind up here?"

"I . . . I don't know how to answer that, sir."

"Why not? Everybody else in this room knows why they're here." Joe turns to our table. "Jon, tell Garrett why you're here."

"Yes, sir." Jon, a thin blond kid with blinking eyes, pops out of his seat. He has a slight tremor, like a small animal perpetually in fear of larger prey. "I was disrespectful to my mom," he says eagerly. "I sold drugs and stole bikes and skipped school."

"Thank you, Jon."

Jon sits obediently. Joe looks up at me. "Tell us why you're here, Garrett?"

"I suppose I was disrespectful, too . . . sir."

"And *how* do you *suppose* you were disrespectful?"

"I didn't do what my parents wanted me to do, sir."

"And what did they want you to do?"

My thoughts are racing like speed chess. What move can I make? What answer can I give? He can't really expect me to talk about this in front of all these people.

"I'll be glad to tell you in private, sir."

Around the room murmurs sprout and vanish like puffs of smoke from firecrackers. Joe snorts with contempt. "I have news for you, Garrett. There is no 'private' here. No one gets through this program with their pride intact, understand? Your pride goes with the rest of the crap. We tear you down, then build you back the way you should be. And we start with you telling *all* of us why you're here."

"Sir, I'm sure that, given a little more time, I can find a way to explain it."

Joe's face reddens, and he glares so fiercely, I can see the pulse in his forehead. I wish I knew what he's so pissed off about. "You don't get it, do you?" he snarls. "This is some kind of game with you. You think all you got to do is *pretend* to cooperate and you'll be out of here?"

"No, sir."

"Oh *yes*, sir. I see it clear as day. Most definitely *yes*, sir."

I stand straight and keep my eyes on his because that is what he ordered me to do. Joe stares back, and a slight, tight smile creeps onto his lips. "Oh, you're good. Yeah, you really think you got this place wired, don't you?"

"No, sir."

"*Yes*, sir!" Joe shouts, and spittle sprays my face.

"Yes, sir."

Joe presses his twitching nose closer. "Well, which is it, punk? Yes, sir, or no, sir?"

"I don't know, sir. I don't know what you want from me, sir."

"You don't know what I want?" he repeats. "What are you, stupid? I just told you!" Joe swings around to the crowd. "You want to know why Garrett's here? Because he'd stay out all night and wouldn't come home. Because he didn't go to school. Because he lied, he stole money, he took drugs, *and* he was messing around with his teacher, who was eight years older than him."

My face is suddenly hot, and the air in my lungs is too thin to breathe. *What the . . . ?* I can't believe my parents told them all that. What were they thinking? It's no one's business.

Once again Joe is under my chin, his face tilted up at mine close enough that I can smell the flowery scent of his hair gel. "You want *me* to tell you why you're here? Because you were disrespectful, disobedient, ignorant, and rebellious. You were ruining your life and your parents' lives, and you were too damn selfish and self-centered to care. Am I right, Garrett?"

My hands ball into fists. My heart is beating hard and my breaths are coming out short and fast. They play by a different set of rules here, and I'd better learn them fast. Out of the corner of my eye I see two black-shirted chaperones moving toward us. That's when it hits me: This is a set up. Joe is trying to get me to take a swing at him. *"The type and degree of restraint administered shall be at the discretion of the staff. Lake Harmony and its employees will not be held liable for any injury sustained by you during the administration of restraint as it is understood that such injury is the result of willful disobedience on your part."*

I take a step back, unclench my fists, and inhale and exhale deeply. My heart is still beating, but the anger is beginning to drain. "Yes, sir. You're right, sir."

Joe's eyes widen for a moment. He knows he almost had me. He looks past me at the approaching chaperones. "Mr. Sparks. Mr. Gold. Take this punk to TI."

The chaperones are the same two who guarded the door to the windowless room when I first arrived. The tall athletic one and the short troll. At the other tables kids grin and leer as if they're glad I'm being taken away. The girl with the black hair and the sign around her neck is one of the few who doesn't look pleased. Our eyes meet again, and she purses her lips and shakes her head slightly, as if to say she's sorry.

Even though I make no attempt to resist, the troll, Mr. Gold, grabs my left wrist and roughly twists my arm behind my back as if I need to be restrained. Mr. Sparks places his hand firmly around my right biceps. They guide me out of the food hall . . . and into hell.

FIVE

"Lake Harmony has your parents' consent to administer whatever punishment is deemed necessary."

Welcome to TI—Temporary Isolation—where I am forced to lie facedown on the cold concrete floor for twenty-four hours a day except for a few minutes here and there to eat or use the bathroom. After a day your chin becomes sore, your neck muscles cramp, and your knees and ribs grow raw from pressing against the hard floor. After two days parts of your body that shouldn't hurt—your elbows and hips, your lower back—begin to ache.

The concrete has a sour, musty smell. You realize

that dozens—no, probably hundreds—of other kids have lain on this very same spot. Is it their sweat you smell, or are you imagining it? Is this the same spot where they placed their faces? Thoughts like this fill me with revulsion, as I can't escape the sense that I'm lying on the germs, the sweat, the smells of the hundreds who've lain here before.

And that's only a small part of the torture. What's far worse is the mental torment. First there's the monotony. Day after day, hour after hour, alone with your thoughts. Perhaps if you were sent to Lake Harmony because you dealt drugs or robbed somebody or stole a car, they would expect you to reflect on the error of your ways and see the mistakes you've made. But what if you haven't done anything seriously wrong, what then?

Only it's not really about what I think is right or wrong, is it? My parents sent me here because it's about what *they* think. And that's a different story. School may have come easily to me; learning to live in my parents' world was much harder. There it seemed that I was always making mistakes. School was black and white. You either knew the answer or you didn't. You were either right or wrong. In my parents' world black was sometimes white, but sometimes it was another color altogether.

On the floor in TI these painful memories stand out like thorns on the stem of a rose. Like the time I was eight and we were having dinner at my father's club. I was wearing my club "uniform"—blue blazer, white shirt, gray slacks. The only opportunity for self-expression came with my choice of ties. That night, I'd chosen a green bow tie.

"You know I don't like that bow tie," said my mother, who was wearing a red dress and white pearls.

"Oh, come on," said my father. "He's just experimenting."

The Frampsons, a family we knew, entered the dining room. Most of the women in my mother's circle were so thin you might think they were emaciated. But Mrs. Frampson was the exception—plump, though certainly not fat. My mother leaned toward my father and me. Her streaked blond hair brushed across the rim of her wine glass. "Look at Hallie Frampson. She just had thousands of dollars' worth of plastic surgery. I don't think it did a bit of good."

Then she waved and smiled at the Frampsons, who came toward our table. As was the custom at the clubs we belonged to, my parents and I rose to greet them. Males shook hands with males. Females kissed females and males on both cheeks.

"Hallie, you look wonderful," my mother gushed.

The Frampsons stayed and chatted for a moment, then moved on. My parents and I sat down again.

"Why did you tell her she looked wonderful?" I asked. "A second ago you said all that plastic surgery didn't do a bit of good."

My mother's cheeks turned bright red as she stared past me. I turned and saw Hallie Frampson standing only a few feet away. She'd stopped to say hello to someone at the table behind us. Obviously, she'd heard what I'd said. Now her hands rose to her face and she rushed toward the ladies' room.

"You little brat," my mother snapped, then jumped up and hurried to the ladies' room to make amends.

You little brat . . . The words stung worse than the hardest slap, mainly because I didn't understand what I'd done wrong. But that was only the beginning.

When I was nine years old and in third grade at the "prestigious" Governor's School, we were assigned to write about our parents' jobs. This is what I wrote:

My father is a lawyer who works on mergers and acquisitions. He helps companies buy other companies. Suppose Bob's Ice Cream Company wants to raise the price of its ice cream to $5 a quart. The problem is Max's Ice Cream Company sells its ice cream for $4 a quart. Bob's is worried that if it raises the price, its customers will switch to Max's. So Bob's hires my father to help them buy Max's company. Once Bob's owns Max's it can charge whatever it wants for its ice cream.

My mother runs a crisis management firm. She helps companies and people who are in trouble. Suppose Tom's Construction Company builds a building that falls down and kills a bunch of people. The relatives of the people who died tell the newspapers they think the building fell down because Tom didn't build it right. But Tom thinks the building fell down because Mary's Brick Company sold them bad bricks. So Tom hires my mom's company to make sure the newspapers know that it was Mary's fault, not his. Or suppose a famous actress gets caught shoplifting. She's worried the bad publicity will ruin her career, so she hires my mom's company to explain that she accidentally took the wrong medicine and didn't know what she was doing.

I got an A. Back then I always got As. But even the As weren't enough. At home my father thought the essay was funny, but my mom got mad because she said it made what she did sound too simple. And besides, she said, I should have written about her first and my dad second because she owned her own company while my dad worked for someone else.

To fight the monotony and boredom of TI, I begin to relive memories: the day I walked into math class and saw Sabrina for the first time, in a red short-sleeved dress, writing an equation on the board; the first time we met outside of school; the first kiss; the first time we made love; and then every time after that.

When I run out of those memories, I recall family vacations—Caribbean beaches, snow-covered mountains in British Columbia, Italian museums— day by day and then hour by hour. I play songs in my head. Then entire CDs, track by track. Then movies, especially my favorites, scene by scene. All this helps, but not enough. Sooner or later an ache or a sudden hunger pang or a full bladder brings me back, and once again I am lying on the cold, hard floor aware of every second grinding slowly past.

"Tell us what you learned in TI, Garrett," Joe orders.

A week or so later a dozen of us are seated in a circle of orange plastic chairs in a small room. In fact, this session is called Circle. A brown curtain is drawn over the only window, and the walls are bare, as if to make sure we have nothing to look at except each other. Half the kids are males from my family. The other half are females from the Truth family. As far as I know, this is the only time males and females are allowed to mix at Lake Harmony.

The girl with the black hair and clear blue eyes is in this group. She is still wearing that sign around her neck.

I slowly rise to my feet. Various parts of my body still hurt, and my back is stiff. "It was extremely unpleasant, sir." My voice sounds strange to me. This is the first time I've spoken in I don't know how many days.

"I don't care what you *thought* of it," Joe snaps. "I asked what you *learned* from it."

What did I learn from TI? That it takes about four days for a caffeine headache to finally go away. That a foot or a hand can go numb and tingly for no apparent reason other than lack of use. That when too many thoughts press in on you, one way to escape is to focus all your attention on each individual breath.

"I learned that it's really uncomfortable to lie facedown on the floor for a week, sir."

Around the room kids snigger. Most of them are still faces without names.

Joe's nose twitches, though his eyes aren't as puffy

or red as before. "What else did you learn?" he asks.

"I don't know, sir."

"You don't know?" Joe repeats, taunting. "I thought you were a smart guy, Garrett. How can you not know?"

"I don't know what you want me to say, sir."

Joe squints and sets his jaw as if he's getting angry. I wonder if it's real anger or just an act. "Boy, you must either be stupider than we thought or a damn masochist to give me that answer. Don't you remember why you got sent to TI in the first place?"

"Send him back," says a thin kid with short brown hair and a face covered with bumpy zits. He sits hunched over, a finger between his lips, gnawing on a fingernail.

I expect Joe to yell at him for speaking out of turn, but my "father" just gazes at me, waiting for my answer.

"You said I had to learn to obey authority, sir."

"And did you?"

"Yes, sir, I did."

"Liar," spits a chubby, red-cheeked girl with stringy brown hair.

"Send him back," repeats Zitface Boy.

A stocky guy with short black hair, deep-set eyes, and thick black eyebrows that meet in the center of his forehead glowers at me. "You are full of crap."

Thus I discover that in Circle we are allowed to speak out as long as what we say shows support for the group leader. Meanwhile, the girl with the black hair widens her eyes and gives me an alarmed look, as if trying to warn me that I'm headed for trouble.

"So there was a time when you didn't obey authority?" asks Joe.

"I guess that depends on your definition of authority, sir."

"I define authority as p-a-r-e-n-t-s." Joe spells the word out. "In your case, parents who expected you to come home at night, go to school during the day, not take drugs, not steal money, and listen to what they said."

"Sir, with all due respect? I went to school enough to make the honor roll. I only smoked once in a while, and the money I took wasn't even pocket change to them."

"That's not what your parents said," Joe replies.

"Can parents ever be wrong, sir?" I ask. "Or, sir, more precisely, if our parents weren't paying for us to be here, *then* could they ever be wrong?"

The kids in Circle go quiet. The question has struck something inside each of them. As if they've all wondered or wanted to ask the same thing at one time or another. Joe instantly shoots them a warning look.

Sitting next to me the red-haired kid with the freckles and the lizard teeth snorts loudly with ridicule. "That's phat."

"Yeah, right!" chimes Chubby Girl, her eyes darting toward Joe for approval.

A noisy chorus of antagonism follows as kids eagerly jump at the opportunity to show Joe that they know better. That they've learned the lesson I'm still struggling with.

"Of course our parents were right, you jerk!"

"Come on, idiot, when are you gonna take responsibility?"

"You can't go through life blaming everyone else when you're the one at fault!"

As each of them recites another patented Lake Harmony slogan—their personal pledge of allegiance—they look to their all-knowing "father" for brownie points.

"Just a perfect little angel," adds glowering Unibrow Boy. "Never had a problem with no one. Doesn't even know why he's here. It must be some kind of mistake." Like the red-haired kid, he radiates an aura of danger.

"Sit down, Garrett," Joe barks. "Suppose I told you that as soon as we're finished with Circle, you're going back to TI? Think that would change your mind?"

"How, sir?" I ask.

Joe stares at me in disbelief, and now I'm pretty sure it's no act. "You really don't get it, do you?"

"He's too stupid," says the red-haired one with the lizard teeth.

"Nah, he thinks he's too smart," counters Zitface. "Just because you memorized the bible doesn't mean you learned it!"

"You haven't learned squat," growls Unibrow.

"Yeah," agrees Chubby Girl. "Send him back to TI."

As if once wasn't enough, the kids in Circle unleash a second barrage of ridicule. It is all, I suspect, designed to curry favor with Joe and earn the points required to move up to the next level and the tiny freedoms that come with it. The wave of abusive shouts and insults all blends together into white noise. But under it I hear someone speaking in my ear. It's the red-haired kid leaning close. "I am gonna mess you up, big guy," he says in a low voice. "Got it? TI is nothing compared to what I am gonna do to you."

What is this? I wonder, turning to face him. He glares back menacingly, his little yellow lizard teeth bared. Why is he threatening me? Under the freckles his skin looks pasty, as if the blood doesn't circulate properly. Maybe there's not enough of it going to his brain.

Meanwhile, Joe allows the verbal abuse to flow for a while, then yells at the others to shut up. Like well-trained dogs, they instantly obey.

"Let's talk about Sabrina," Joe says.

At the unexpected sound of her name, I feel myself flinch. Sabrina. Her deep brown eyes and soft brown hair. The exotic scent of her almond skin. Where is she at this very moment? What is she doing? By now she must know that I've been sent away. Is she sitting at the computer, under the Hockney pool poster I gave her, waiting for my IM to appear? Does she check the mailbox each day for a letter I'm not allowed to write? The ache I feel for her is greater than any physical pain. Lying on the floor in TI, I replayed conversations we'd had. Recalled her smell, her touch, the way her hair fell into her face, the way she giggled, and groaned, and would sometimes wrap her arms around my chest and squeeze as if knowing that someday some invisible force would pull us apart.

"Garrett!" Joe harshly pulls me out of those

memories. "You want to go back to TI right now, or you want to talk?"

Why is he doing this? Doesn't anyone else get a chance to be skewered? Across from me the girl with the black hair raises her blue eyes curiously.

"Sabrina," Joe prompts me.

"She's . . . a woman I know . . . sir."

"A *woman*," Chubby Girl repeats, scornfully, as if she assumes I'm being pretentious. She must not have heard what Joe said in the food hall before they sent me to TI. Not far from her, a pale and delicate boy with blond hair, blue eyes, and pouty lips leans forward as if trying to hear better.

"That's all you have to say?" Joe asks. "Nothing about her being eight years older than you? Or that she was your teacher? Or that you repeatedly disobeyed your parents, who forbade you to see her?"

This time there are no jeers. The kids gaze at the walls and floor with uncertain expressions, as if they're not sure what to think. The pale blond boy stares at me with a look of wonder and curiosity.

"Gee, it sounds like maybe you do have a problem with authority," Joe says.

"I believe that's different, sir."

His nose twitches. "Different? How?"

"I love her, sir."

The room remains silent for what feels like a long time. Until next to me the red-haired kid smirks. "Aw, how cute."

"Shut up, Adam!" The girl with the black hair jumps down his throat.

"If your parents forbid you to do something and you repeatedly disobey them," Joe says, "how is that different?"

"They don't understand, sir," I answer. "I tried to explain it to them a hundred times."

"No!" Joe disagrees harshly. "*You're* the one who doesn't understand. You are a *child*. They are your parents. You don't know what's best for you. They do. You are to obey them unconditionally. That is precisely why you are here, Garrett. And you will stay here until you learn that. Do you understand?"

I lower my head and stare at my bare toes in my flip-flops. What I understand is that I've always related better to adults than to kids my own age. It's not exactly something I'm proud of. Believe me, it would have been a lot easier the other way around. But from the time I was young, I was like an older person trapped in a kid's body. While other kids were reading Goosebumps, I was reading Stephen King. When they were listening to hip-hop, I was into jazz. While they were watching teenage horror movies, I was watching the films of Martin Scorsese and Paul Haggis.

Then I met Sabrina, and there was an instant connection. I'd never felt anything like it. At first the eight-year difference in age felt strange. I admit it bothered her a lot more than me. But she looked younger than her age, while I, more than six feet tall and shaving every day, seemed older. Strangers never questioned seeing us together. We looked like a couple in our late teens.

But it wasn't just outward appearances. I felt we

were meant to be together. We were both math geeks and manga heads. Every time Sabrina started to fret that being with me was wrong, that people her age weren't supposed to have "intimate relations" with people my age, I pointed out that there used to be laws against relations between people of different races, or of the same sex. We now think of those laws as barbaric or uninformed.

People develop at different speeds. I told her over and over that sometimes the "normal" rules don't apply. She tried suggesting that we wait until I turned eighteen. But to me that sounded like an eternity.

"Garrett, I asked you if you understood," Joe repeats.

I understand that I'm a prisoner in a place where my parents are paying a lot of money to get other people to do what they've been unable to do. Which is convince me that something that feels completely right is wrong.

"Well?" Joe says.

"Yes, sir, I understand."

"What do you understand?"

"I understand . . . that I will stay here . . . until I learn, sir."

"Learn what?"

"That I must obey my parents unconditionally, sir."

Once again the room grows quiet. Until Chubby Girl says, "Don't believe him. He's full of it."

And for once, she's right.

SIX

"You will be observed by a staff member or student guard at all times."

"See those lights in the ceiling?" Joe asks. It's Shut Down, and we are in the dorm where Dignity family sleeps. The day at Lake Harmony starts at six A.M. We run and do drills until eight A.M. and then wash up for breakfast at eight-thirty. After breakfast we study in classrooms until lunch. After lunch we have more studies, then more drills, then Circle. After that comes dinner, then Reflections, and then at nine-thirty P.M. we wash once again and prepare for Shut Down at ten.

The dorm walls are bare gray cinder blocks, and there are no windows, just a door at one end and an open doorway to the bathroom at the other. The air in here is hot and stinks of stale teenage sweat. Sixteen metal cots in two rows of eight are jammed into the room, plus four additional mattresses that go on the floor each night. The other members of Dignity stand in neat rows in front of their cots or mattresses, listening while Joe yells at me.

"Are you stupid, Garrett? I asked you a question!" he shouts, sending spittle into my face.

"Yes, sir, I see those lights." On the ceiling above the cots are two rows of tiny red lights, but I'm thinking about those four mattresses on the floor. They are reserved for the Level Ones, but the mattresses aren't punishment. There's simply no space for more cots in this room. When Lake Harmony makes four thousand dollars a month on each kid, those four extra mattresses add up to nearly two hundred thousand extra dollars a year.

"Garrett!" Joe screams.

Spittle hits my face again, but I dare not wipe it away. I am a Level One. I am not allowed to move without permission.

"Yes, sir."

"Pay attention, you dumb ass. Those are motion detectors. You get out of bed in the middle of the night, they go off. You can use the bathroom once before Shut Down; then you stay in bed until morning."

"Yes, sir," I answer, even though I have no bed. I am one of the lowly who sleep on a mattress on the floor.

"Even if you were to somehow get out of this room, there are motion detectors in the halls," Joe continues.

"And the panic bars on the doors to the outside are wired to lock automatically for forty-five seconds if touched."

Joe must see the confusion on my face.

"What's the problem?" he barks.

"What if there's a fire, sir?"

"That's why they lock for only forty-five seconds, you idiot. Any more stupid questions?"

"No, sir."

Joe moves down the line to the pale, delicate boy with blond hair and blue eyes. The boy's shoulders are stooped, and he begins to tremble when Joe stops in front of him. The boy's bare arms and neck are covered by a patchy, oozing, reddish rash.

"What is that, Pauly?" Joe asks in a disgusted tone.

"I don't know, sir," Pauly answers in a quavering voice.

"You don't know?" Joe asks. "It's a rash, you dumb wimp. You ever have anything like that before?"

"Well, a couple of times, when I ate something that disagreed with me, sir."

"Something that *disagreed* with you?" Joe repeats with revulsion. He turns to the rest of us. "You hear that, boys? Little Pauly ate something that disagreed with him. Oh, iddn't dat jus too, too bad?" He finishes in baby talk.

A few kids grin. Others eye Pauly with looks of utter derision.

"Now lemme ax you someting, wittle Pauwy," Joe continues in the humiliating baby talk. "Are you sure you ate someting dat disagweed wit your wittle tummy? Or maybe you just wubbed yourself against the wall to make it look like a waash so you could have a wittle vacation in the infirmawee."

Still trembling, Pauly shakes his head and stares down at the floor, blinking hard to fight back tears.

"I didn't hear your answer, wittle Pauwy," Joe says mockingly.

A tear drops off Pauly's eyelid and splats on the floor. His lower lip quivers. The kid has a rash. Why is Joe tormenting him? It takes every muscle in my body not to shout at Joe to lay off.

"What's a matter, wittle Pauwy, can't you talk?" Joe taunts.

"I . . . I didn't rub against anything."

"What?" Joe snaps sharply.

Pauly jumps. "Sir!"

"So wittle Pauwy didn't wub against anyting," Joe goes on. "He just ate someting dat disagweed wit him. Well, dat's too bad, wittle Pauwy, but you're not going anywhere near the infirmawee. You'll just have to tough it out and get better all by your wittle self."

It hardly seems to matter that Pauly never asked to go to the infirmary.

Having reduced Pauly to a jellylike blob of tears, Joe leaves. But we are not left alone. In addition to frequent check-ins by the chaperones, the Level Five and Six kids become "teen guards" at night. Just before Shut Down they escort us two at a time to the bathroom and watch while we use the toilets, which are in stalls without doors. The teen guards then take turns staying up at night, reporting every infraction to Joe in the morning. So it seems strange to me when, shortly after Joe leaves, Adam brushes close to Pauly and mutters something. Pauly hangs his head and follows him to the end of the room, where the two of them disappear into the bathroom.

A moment later they are followed by Zitface. I've learned that his name is David and he's a Level Four. Unibrow Robert, the stocky Level Three with the dark eyebrows, also goes. This appears to be an obvious violation of the rules, but the two Level Five guards, Ron and Jon, continue preparing for bed as if nothing unusual is happening. Even when the sounds of a scuffle come from the bathroom, the others pretend they hear nothing. There's a loud slap, followed by a muffled cry. Slaps are favored at Lake Harmony because they leave no telltale bruises in the morning.

"Aahh!" A sharper yelp of pain comes from the bathroom. The rest of us in the dorm share furtive looks. It's three against one in there, and the one is weak and defenseless.

"Ow!"

The hell with the stupid Lake Harmony rules. I head toward the bathroom, but teen guard Ron blocks my path and says, "Don't."

"They're hurting him for no reason."

"Go to bed or I'll tell Joe," Ron warns.

I point toward the bathroom. "You gonna tell Joe about what's going on in there?"

Ron doesn't react. It's almost like he didn't hear the question. "That's none of your business."

I step around him and head toward the bathroom.

Behind me Ron threatens, "You're in big trouble."

In the bathroom Adam has backed Pauly against the wall, one hand jammed against the kid's throat, the other holding something thin and light blue under Pauly's nose. It's a toothbrush that's been scraped down into a pointed weapon. In prisons they're called shivs. David Zitface and Unibrow Robert stand nearby, watching with amused leers.

"Let him go."

Adam and his posse spin around with startled expressions. "Get lost," Adam snarls. What makes him the leader? He can't be more than 5'9", and he's narrowly built, and slouches. Clearly, the power he wields must be psychological.

I stand with my arms crossed. "I said, let him go."

With one hand still on Pauly's neck, Adam aims the shiv at me. "You want to get messed up bad?"

The threat sounds hollow, so I don't answer. I just wait.

Adam gestures with his little plastic weapon. "I said get lost."

When I still don't move, David Zitface and Unibrow Robert shoot nervous looks at Adam, who frowns uncertainly and points at Pauly. "What do you care about this piece of dirt?"

"He's not a piece of dirt," I reply patiently. "And this isn't some prison movie. What are you doing to him?"

Adam lets go of Pauly, who slides down the wall until he's sitting on the floor, knees pulled into his chest, sobbing.

Adam gazes down contemptuously. "I don't see a human being. I see a piece of crybaby crap that doesn't deserve to live."

"What's with you?" I ask. "You sound like you're reading a script. How would you like it if I did that to you?"

"Fat chance," Adam scoffs.

When you're big, you learn to use your body in carefully measured ways. A half step in Adam's direction and a slight tilt of the forehead show everyone what my intentions are. "Leave him alone."

Adam steps away from Pauly and jabs the shiv in my direction, but he's now clearly on the defensive. "I'll kick your ass in so many ways, you won't know night from day," he warns. But his voice is a tremulous octave higher than before, and he and his little gang start to leave the bathroom.

I step to the side, giving them room to pass. They go, grimacing and gnarling like dogs on a leash. Adam is the last, and as he passes, he aims the pointed end of the toothbrush at me. "You're a dead man."

SEVEN

"You may be placed in Temporary Isolation at any time for any reason."

"Take Garrett to TI, Mr. Gold," Joe says the next morning.

"But sir, what about what Adam did to Pauly?" I ask, while the troll grabs my wrist and twists my arm hard behind my back to make sure I cooperate.

"I don't know what you're talking about," Joe replies. "Ron and Jon, come with us."

I glance at Pauly, who hangs his head and won't meet my gaze. If he talks, it's a death sentence.

Keeping my arm behind my back, the troll walks me down the hall. Joe follows, spewing his nonstop litany of abuse. "You still don't get it, Garrett. You think you're smart, but you're too stupid to see how it works here. You have no rights. Your opinions don't count. You're just a punk kid with a crap attitude, and you don't know squat. When are you gonna figure out that what you think doesn't matter? The only things that matter are what I think and what your parents think. That's why you're here, Garrett. Because you didn't listen to your parents. And that's what you're going to think about in TI, dimwit. Learning to listen. Learning to obey. Learning to do what your parents say."

The troll shoves me into the TI room and follows with Ron and Jon. Joe remains in the doorway.

"No marks," Joe says, and closes the door.

"Face down on the floor," the troll orders.

I do as I'm told, and then Jon and Ron get to work. They spit and slap and twist and squeeze. Everything that hurts but will leave no telltale bruises tomorrow. I grit my teeth, trying not to let them have the satisfaction of knowing how much pain I'm in, but grunts and yelps escape my lips whenever the stabbing, twisting agony becomes too great. They grind the heels of their shoes into my knees and elbows. Only Level Ones through Fours are required to wear flip-flops, allegedly to slow us down in case we try to run away. Level Fives and Sixes are rewarded by being allowed to wear shoes.

"Stop!" I hear myself cry when Ron twists my arm so hard, it feels like it will explode out of the shoulder socket.

Standing near the door with his arms folded and a demented smile on his lips, the troll asks, "What's the matter, Garrett? Can't take a little pain?"

"I'd like to see you take it."

"WHAT?" the troll shouts. At the same moment Ron twists my arm harder.

"Sorry, sir!" I instantly apologize and feel relief as Ron eases up.

"You better be," the troll murmurs.

The beating stops, and I feel my aching body go limp. *Sabrina, if you knew what I'm going through . . .*

"Good work, boys." The troll praises Ron and Jon as they leave, and the door slams and locks. So this is how they do it here. The staff can't be accused of harming kids because they have other kids do it for them. And why would Ron and Jon agree? Because you don't get out of Lake Harmony unless you prove whose side you're on.

"You deserve to be here."

"Everything you did before was wrong."

"You'll never leave until you learn to respect authority."

"Change your attitude to gratitude. Your parents sent you here to save you. You owe them everything."

Each day I hear these chants when Ron and Jon come back to slap and twist and spit. By now I've lost track of how long I've been in TI. Jon and Ron are like robot zombies. They drone the words with no feeling, as if they're reciting a mantra. The troll usually accompanies them for my daily beatings. But today for some reason he's not here.

"You suck, Gary Durrell." Jon leans a knee into the

small of my back. "You're stupid, pathetic, and good for nothing. Just a miserable excuse for being human."

"Are you even listening to what you're saying?" I ask, twisting my head around and looking up at him. "You just called me Gary. My name's Garrett."

Above me Jon blinks. Both he and Ron pause from their "duties." I roll over onto my elbows and look up at them. "Seriously, what are you guys doing?"

If ever there was a moment when one of them might have said something that showed they were faking or pretending just to get out of this place, now would be it. But instead Jon answers robotically: "You have to renounce your old ways."

"You deserved to be sent here," Ron adds. "We're trying to help you."

"You guys really have been brainwashed," I tell them.

The word detonates something in Jon. *Smack!* He slaps me hard in the face. "You better stop mouthing off, loser."

"You gotta admit you have anger issues," Ron says.

Anger issues?

And for the rest of the session they beat me extra hard.

The door to TI opens, and Joe comes in with Mr. Sparks.

"Get up, you worthless piece of crap."

I rise slowly. My body aches from the daily torture. Feeling light-headed and dizzy, I have to put my hands on my knees and bend at the waist to keep from passing out.

Whack! Joe smacks me across the back of the head. "Straighten up!"

I slowly obey his command. Joe steps close and stares up at me as if reading my eyes. "Nope, you still don't get it. Still think you don't belong here, right?"

There's no answer I can give that will satisfy him. Without warning he drives his fist into my stomach, knocking the wind out of me. I double over, gasping in pain.

"When I ask a question, you answer," he barks.

It takes me a moment to catch my breath.

"Well?"

"If I answer, you'll just hit me again, sir."

Pow! He hits me anyway.

Still in TI. The places where my body takes my weight on the floor—elbows, knees, hips, ribs—have grown excruciatingly sore. In this windowless room I lose track of day and night; I merely doze on and off. Immeasurable lumps of time float past. To escape the numbing sameness, I retreat to the land of memories:

My dad and me rafting down the Colorado River, bucking the rapids, the cold water splashing my face, my hands gripping the safety ropes.

Sabrina and me spending four dollars on a truffle in a chocolate shop. The taste of chocolate and raspberry on my tongue. Then tasting it again on Sabrina's lips.

Lying on my bed at home, ears encased in Sennheiser headphones, listening to music with the volume so high that the sound has a heavy, syrupy quality . . .

Another week passes. Or maybe it's only three days. Ron and Jon come in to deliver another beating. What scares me the most is knowing they really believe what they're doing. I don't know what happened in their lives before they got here, but they've become devoted disciples of the philosophy of Lake Harmony.

Because school came easily, I was often bored. Even in accelerated math the teacher would introduce a concept—converting fractions to percentages, for example—and I would get it right away. Then, while she was explaining it to the rest of the class, I would finish that night's homework assignment.

My parents complained that they never saw me doing any homework, and yet I always got the highest grades in the class. They asked if I could skip a grade, but the headmaster said it was important that I stay with my peer group. My dad suggested I go to a different school, but the Governor's School was the fanciest in the city and my mom liked telling people I went there.

At the age of twelve I stayed home for a week with strep throat. Back in school it only took a day or two to catch up and learn everything I'd missed. That's when I realized I didn't have to go every day.

"You have to go to school, Garrett," my father said one night after receiving a call from the headmaster that I'd missed two days that week. My mother wasn't there. She was working late, as usual.

"I do go to school," I answered.

"*Every day,*" my father stressed.

"Why?"

"Because you're supposed to," he said.

"I thought I'm supposed to get good grades so I can go to a good college," I said.

"That too," said my father.

"But I don't need to go to school every day to do that," I said.

"You still have to go every day," he insisted.

"Why?"

"Because you do."

"Because" wasn't enough for me. People got into college based on their grades, not on how often they attended school. Besides, there were other, more interesting things to do: museums to visit; neighborhoods to walk through, where the air was fragrant with the smells of exotic foods; old men in the park to play chess with; construction sites to explore. If it only took me two or three days a week to learn what other kids needed five for, why did I have to sit around and be bored?

EIGHT

"You will share the intimate details of your life."

The door opens, and Mr. Sparks, the athletic, dark-skinned chaperone, comes in.

"Time to go, Garrett."

"Where?" I ask in a daze.

"Where, *sir*," he corrects me.

"Sorry, sir."

Mr. Sparks checks his watch. "Circle."

I rise slowly and stiffly from the floor. Out in the hallway my balance is so unsteady that I weave like a drunk and have to press my hands against the walls like a sailor in a storm. My legs feel weak from disuse. The air in the hallway feels warm and sticky. Through a small window I can see that the trees are covered with dark green leaves. A female with short brown hair lumbers across the field, carrying a car tire under each arm. She trips and falls face first to the ground. The tires bounce away and flop over. An upper-level female (same red polo shirt, but longer hair) screams at her to get up. Still peering through the window as I walk, I accidentally bang my shoulder turning the corner.

"Easy, Garrett," Mr. Sparks says with a hint of amusement. "Don't want to hurt yourself after all that."

Something about the tone of his voice makes me wonder if I should take a chance. "Can I ask how long I was in TI, sir?"

Mr. Sparks doesn't answer right away. He's walking behind me, and I don't dare turn around to see the expression on his face. We both know I've broken the rule against talking.

Relief washes through me when Mr. Sparks drops his voice and says, "A while."

"How come they let me out, sir?"

"Guess they need the room for someone else."

"How many Temporary Isolation rooms are there, sir?"

He doesn't answer. We're getting closer to our destination, but there's one more question I need to ask. "Sir, how do you get out of this place?"

"Give them what they want, Garrett," Mr. Sparks answers in a solemn whisper, then steps past me and knocks on the door to circle.

Joe opens it. The red puffiness around his eyes has

receded, and his nose no longer twitches. "Well, look who's here," he says with a sinister smile. "You miss us, Garrett?"

"Yes, sir," I answer. It's probably the first time he's asked a question I could give an honest answer to. After all those days alone, it's good to see anyone who isn't there to hurt me.

"Come on in."

Inside, Pauly greets me with a weak smile. He looks pale and thinner than before. The rash has spread over more of his body, but it isn't as deep-red or oozy. Now it's more pink in color. Lizard Teeth Adam and his henchmen David Zitface and Unibrow Robert are there.

A somber-looking girl sits next to Pauly. Her hair has been chopped into a ragged, uneven crew cut, as if it was done by a child with scissors. Her skin is so pasty, it's almost green. With a start I realize it's the girl who used to wear the sign around her neck. Her eyes, once so clear and blue, are now empty and sunken. Her arms are covered with Band-Aids and gauze pads held in place by white adhesive tape.

"Take a seat, Garrett," Joe orders, then turns to the others. "Where were we?"

"Sarah, sir," Adam reminds him.

"Right." Joe nods grimly. "So what's it been, Sarah? Two and a half years?"

Sarah, the girl with the chopped black hair, stares down at the floor.

"I'm talking to you, Sarah," Joe barks.

She looks up, and, as if mustering every last bit of

energy she has, says, "What are you going to do next, Joe? Kill me? I don't think my parents will keep paying four thousand dollars a month once I'm dead."

The disrespect in her voice is shocking. By Lake Harmony standards she should be blindfolded and shot. But strangely, Joe doesn't react.

"You've already lost two and a half years of your life," he replies in a measured tone. "You might as well have been dead all that time. And for what? All because you think you know more than your parents."

"I never said that," Sarah answers. "I just don't agree with what they believe. You can't *make* someone believe."

"If you can't believe, you can show respect," Joe says.

"Come on, Joe," Sarah says with a tired sigh. "We've been over this a hundred times. What's the point?"

"The point is, maybe if you go over it enough, it'll sink into that stupid brain," says Unibrow Robert.

"Talk about stupid brains," Sarah shoots back. "I'm not the one who got sent here for huffing glue."

"Then how come I'm almost Level Four and you're still Level One?" Robert asks.

"Everybody knows why you're almost Level Four," Sarah grumbles.

"Because I've learned that the person I used to be was a real jerk," Robert claims. "When I get out, I'm not gonna be that person again. I'm gonna be a new person. A better person. Something you'll never be."

"You are so full of it," Sarah snorts. "Just repeating what Joe wants to hear doesn't prove anything. Being part of Adam's little gestapo may help you rise through the levels, but it doesn't make you a better person."

Robert scowls, and Sarah is quick to figure out why. "The gestapo was Hitler's secret police," she explains. "I assume you know who Hitler was. Or am I still giving you too much credit?"

All you have to see is the imploring look Robert gives Joe to know everything Sarah just said is true.

"I'm thinking about what you said before, Sarah," Joe says patiently. "Maybe you're right. Maybe you will die here. But it won't be because of anything any of us do. You're doing it to yourself."

NINE

"You must earn the right to speak."

"You can't win."

On this hot and humid early summer day seven of us are squatting before white plastic buckets in a gravel area near the parking lot. Birds chirp in the trees, and dragonflies flit back and forth overhead. We're washing our clothes, but the sky is a thick gray haze, and when we spread them out on the gravel, they just lie there wet and don't dry. Clotheslines are not allowed. Rope of any sort is forbidden at Lake Harmony.

"Kids die here."

Until a few moments ago there were ten of us, but Adam and two other guys got into a scuffle when one of them accidentally knocked over Adam's bucket. Joe and Mr. Sparks dragged them away, leaving the rest of us in the hands of Ron and Jon. But they're across the parking lot, rinsing buckets with a hose.

"A kid died two years ago." The one talking is Pauly, the frail blond boy.

"Shut up," snarls David Zitface.

Pauly ignores him. "I'm going to die here. It's been a year and nine months and I'm still Level One."

"Can it, Pauly," hisses a dark-skinned boy named Stu. "Ron and Jon catch you talking, we'll all get in trouble."

"Why will *you* get in trouble?" I ask Stu.

"Christ, not you too, Garrett," Stu says with a sigh. "You're not supposed to talk. I'm a Level Three. I see you breaking a rule, I'm supposed to turn you in. You get caught talking and they know I heard you and didn't turn you in, then I'll get demerits. It's my butt that's on the line."

Ignoring him, Pauly continues: "You want to know why I'm here?"

"For God's sake, Pauly, if you gotta talk, at least whisper!" Stu beseeches under his breath.

"Back off," Pauly says. "I'm talking to Garrett."

White buckets filled with sudsy water scrape over the gravel as Stu and some of the other boys inch away. By disregarding the rules Pauly threatens to drag them all down. On the other hand, as Level Ones, he and I risk nothing except a trip to TI. But why is Pauly so willing to get in trouble just to talk to me?

"I'm here because I'm not the son my father

wanted," Pauly continues. "He wanted a big, strong kid like you."

"Instead he got a freakin' faggot who can't keep his mouth closed," David Zitface growls as he slides his bucket farther from us.

"If my dad found out I was having an affair with an older woman, he'd be thrilled," says Pauly.

"I wonder why," sniggers Unibrow Robert.

"Everyone thinks I'm gay," says Pauly, "but I'm not. I think about girls all the time. I have wet dreams about them."

"Whoa, that's *way* more information than we need," says David Zitface.

By now the other guys have dragged their buckets at least thirty feet from us. Pauly keeps his head turned away from them. "Think they can still hear me?" he suddenly whispers.

I shake my head ever so slightly. But what's he up to?

"Okay, listen up, this is serious," Pauly whispers with unexpected urgency. "You and I are *never* gonna get out of here. You're kidding yourself if you think you can graduate by just obeying the rules and saying you're sorry for what you did before. You have to *believe* it. That's what they do here. They indoctrinate you to the Lake Harmony way of thinking. It's something you can't fake."

Pauly's words spill out in a rush of conviction, as if he's been waiting weeks to say them. "You see Jon and Ron? They're not faking. It's brainwashing, and it works on a lot of these kids because they *have* done something wrong. They've done drugs and broken the law and all kinds of crap."

He pauses and studies me. "Okay, don't answer. You're smart. As long as they don't see you talking, you can't get in trouble. Good thing they haven't figured out how to punish kids for listening. Just give me some kind of sign, like whether you want me to keep talking or go away."

I give him the slightest nod. Guess it can't hurt to hear what he has to say.

"Right. Okay, so how is being in love wrong?" Pauly whispers. "How is being born a weak geek like me wrong? What do they want me to believe? That I'm a frickin' mistake? See, the problem with this place is they take anyone they get. As long as your parents pay the bill, Lake Harmony doesn't care. Your parents sent you here because they want you to be a different person. Mr. Z and company are happy to oblige."

I wonder if Pauly thinks we're friends because I stopped Adam and his gang from beating him in the bathroom. But I would have done that for anyone.

"There's another thing," Pauly goes on. "Some kids think if they wait long enough, someone'll come save them. Like a sister or an uncle or someone. Well, it ain't happening. Your parents signed a confidentiality agreement not to tell anyone where this place is. No one can come get you, because no one except your parents knows where you are."

A crow lands on the gravel a few yards to our left. The large black bird cocks its head and looks at us, then lifts its wings and flaps away. Sabrina has no idea where

I am. What would I have done if she'd been the one who'd suddenly disappeared without warning? Would I have tried to find her? Would I have simply waited for the day she'd return? How long would I have waited?

How long will she wait?

"There's only one answer," Pauly whispers. "We have to get out of here. It's our only chance. And we're not alone. There's another person who'll go with us. Think it over, okay?"

The kid has to be crazy to tell me this. Doesn't he realize I could rat him out and score major points with Joe? Or is this a setup? A trap to see if I'd really be stupid enough to agree to try to escape? Thirty feet away, Stu clears his throat. Joe and Mr. Sparks are walking toward the parking lot. As they near us, Unibrow Robert intercepts them. "Pauly was talking, sir. He said a kid died here two years ago and that he's going to die here. He said if his dad found out he was having a relationship with an older woman, he'd be thrilled."

A laugh bursts uncontrollably from Mr. Sparks's lips, but Joe shoots him a silencing look, and the chaperone covers his mouth with his hand and pretends to cough. Meanwhile, Joe stands over Pauly, who hangs his head, awaiting his sentence.

"Twenty-five push-ups, fifty sit-ups, and a hundred squat thrusts," Joe orders.

Pauly moves slowly away from his bucket. He steps out of his flip-flops and assumes the prone position. He manages to do five push-ups before it becomes an effort. His back dips like an old horse's and his arms tremble.

By the eighth push-up he's dropped to his knees.

"Seventeen more," Joe barks.

It's a struggle. Each push-up is feebler than the last, until Pauly can barely lift his shoulders off the gravel. Next come the sit-ups, the gravel clinging to the back of his polo shirt each time he manages to rise. Like the push-ups, these become more and more pathetic until he needs to prop himself up with his elbows in order to sit.

All the while Joe stands over him, counting. It is, of course, the perfect punishment for the boy whose father wants to toughen him up.

Finally, Pauly completes the sit-ups. Now with bare hands and feet he starts the squat thrusts, slamming the palms of his hands down on the rough, pointy gravel, then kicking his bare feet out behind him. It must be incredibly painful, and by the twentieth squat thrust two toes on his left foot are scraped bloody. Tears run down Pauly's cheeks.

That's when I realize this was no trap. Pauly *knew* he was going to get caught if he talked to me. He knew the punishment would be painful. But that's how badly he wants to get out of here.

Later we line up in the hall before dinner. Pauly is in front of me, shoulders slouched, head hanging, beaten down. In the flip-flops his bare feet are covered with dark scabs and smeared with dried blood. Like animals in a herd knowing instinctually that the weakest member will most likely attract a predator's attack, the others stay as far away from him as they can.

Joe walks down the line and stops beside me. "I hear Pauly had a lot to say this afternoon. Maybe you'd like to fill us in."

"He said his father sent him here because he's not the son he wanted, sir," I reply.

"What else?"

"Lake Harmony will take anyone whose parents are willing to pay, sir."

"What else?"

"I shouldn't think anyone's going to come get me because no one knows where I am."

"What else?"

I pretend to think for a moment. "That's all, sir."

"You sure?"

"Yes, sir."

Now it's Joe's turn to pause. "Step out of line, Garrett."

I do as ordered.

Joe takes a stick of gum out of his shirt pocket and slowly unwraps it. Lake Harmony does not serve dessert or anything sweet, and the minty scent is incredibly tantalizing. Joe waves the stick under my nose before he pops it into his mouth. Then he crumples the wrapper and drops it on the floor.

"Pick it up," he orders.

I bend down and get it. When I straighten back up, Joe holds out his hand, palm upward. But that doesn't mean he wants me to put the wrapper in it.

Joe smiles. "Not bad, Garrett. Now give it to me."

I place it in his palm. He turns his hand over, and the wrapper falls to the floor. "Pick it up."

My eyes meet Joe's. Under the mustache a slightly sadistic smile traces his lips. Once again I bend down and pick up the wrapper, then wait for the next order. Joe tells me to give it to him, and when I do, he drops it. "Pick it up, stupid."

I do what he says.

"Give it to me."

He drops it.

"Pick it up, stupid."

"Give it to me."

"Pick it up, stupid."

"Give it to me."

It's Simon Says for boot-campers. The others watch, some with amusement on their faces, others wincing at the malicious nature of it.

"Pick it up, stupid."

"Give it to me."

"Ahem." Mr. Sparks clears his throat.

Joe checks his watch. "The rest of you, go with Mr. Sparks to dinner."

They march away down the hall while I stay behind with Joe. We're alone now.

"Pick it up, stupid."

"Give it to me."

"Pick it up, stupid."

"Give it to me."

Finally, I make a mistake. He drops the wrapper and I bend to pick it up. *Crunk!* He knees me in the face. Blood gushes out of my nose, dripping onto my shirt. I tilt my head back and pinch the bridge of my nose, but it hardly stops the bleeding. Joe grimaces and steps back.

"I thought you were supposed to be a smart guy, Garrett. Did I tell you to pick it up?"

Still pinching my nose, I answer, "No, sir."

"Then why did you?"

"Made a mistake, sir."

Drip . . . A drop of blood plops to the floor at my feet.

Drip . . . Another drop of blood falls.

Joe stares down with a look of revulsion on his face. But I can't do anything about it.

Drip . . .

Drip . . .

Joe makes a decision.

"All right, pick it up, stupid."

On the floor the wrapper lies among the drops of blood. Pinching my nose with one hand, I reach down with the other. Of course, this starts the blood flowing again. Some gets on the gum wrapper. When I straighten up, Joe is waiting with his palm out. I hold the damp, red, sticky wrapper and wait.

"Give it to me."

But this time he moves his hand so the wrapper falls straight to the floor.

"Pick it up, stupid."

"Give it to me."

Each time I go to drop the wrapper, he moves his hand so that it falls to the floor.

"Pick it up, stupid."

Each time I bend down, the blood gushes from my nose anew. The constant bending and straightening makes me dizzy. I begin to feel light-headed and have to plant my hands on my knees.

"Did I say you could stop?" Joe demands.

"No, sir."

"Then pick it up, stupid."

I reach down for the gum wrapper, which is now lying in a puddle of blood. Suddenly my vision becomes distorted, as if everything is made of Silly Putty and it's being stretched in all directions. The next thing I know, the floor is racing up toward my face.

Thunk!

When I come to, the right side of my face throbs with pain where it must have hit the floor. My chest feels wet, and I realize I'm lying on the puddle of blood. A different kind of pain emanates from my ankle, where Joe is pressing down with the sole of his shoe.

"Did I say you could fall down?"

"No . . . sir."

"Get up."

Still dizzy, my face wet with blood and my shirt sticking to my skin, I slowly rise to my feet. The only good news is that my nose finally seems to have stopped bleeding.

"Pick it up, stupid."

I look down at the smeared streaks and globs of reddish-brown blood coagulating on the floor. The wrapper isn't there. Joe looks down and searches for it. Then he looks up and wrinkles his nose in disgust as he stares at my chest. The gum wrapper is stuck to my shirt with blood-red glue.

I pick the wrapper off and hold it out to him. Joe jerks back as if I just offered him a fresh turd or something. He looks like he's ready to barf.

Something tells me to step toward him.

He steps back. Strange how this is what Lake Harmony is all about: power and domination and fear. They take away our power and it makes us fear them. Why am I not allowed to speak or move without permission? It is a way of stripping away my power of self-expression. When they have all the strength and we have none, we fear them and do whatever they want. TI, the beatings, the humiliation—they're all about leaving us naked and weak and forcing us into subservience.

But oddly, my blood is power. Covered by it, I'm like some horror-movie ghoul. I take another step and feel the balance between Joe and me shift like a seesaw rising and falling.

"Stop!" he orders, his voice a notch higher than before. It's almost as if we're not at Lake Harmony anymore and I'm not a Level One with fewer human rights than a refugee from some third-world civil war. For a moment Lake Harmony's ridiculously tyrannical system of rules and points doesn't apply. Not that I could lose any points anyway, since I have none. I take another step.

"You'll be so sorry," Joe hisses. "You have no frickin' idea what's gonna happen to you."

I stop. "But what's the point, sir? If you beat me until I'm a zombie like Jon and Ron, what does that prove?"

Sensing I won't come closer, Joe breathes a little more easily. "Parents send their kids here because they've lost control. Their kids are self-destructing, and they have no place else to turn. A lot of these kids would be in jail, or strung out, or dead if they weren't here. We save lives, Garrett."

"So Pauly's gonna stay here until he makes the football team, sir?"

"That's up to Pauly's parents, not me," Joe replies. "My job is to make sure Pauly's parents get a kid who'll try out for the football team if that's what they want him to do."

We've reached a stalemate. Covered with blood like this I could probably back him all the way down the hall. At the same time I realize that that is most likely what he expects. Doing it will just reinforce what he already believes about us "completely out of control" kids with all our "anger issues" and "crap attitudes."

So instead I point down at the gummy red mess on the hallway floor. Damned if it doesn't look like a murder scene. You can imagine one of those chalk police outlines where the body lay. "Shouldn't I clean it up, sir?"

Joe cocks an eyebrow suspiciously, as if this must be a trick. He walks a dozen feet, pulls a key ring off his belt, and unlocks some kind of janitor's closet. Inside are mops and brooms, a bucket on wheels, and a sink. He holds the door open for me. "Get to work."

I nod subserviently and reach for the mop and bucket. "Yes, sir."

And suddenly we're back at Lake Harmony.

TEN

"You will not criticize Lake Harmony."

"Go on." The troll points at the concrete steps to the old brick administration building. I climb up and pause at the wooden front door, waiting for the next command.

"Knock and go in," the troll orders.

I do as told. The air in the lobby is cool and air-conditioned. The troll points at the door to Mr. Z's office. I cross the lobby to the door, then stop and look back at him.

"Knock."

I knock.

"Come in," the gruff voice says.

Inside, the office is even cooler than in the lobby.

Mr. Z is sitting at his desk, studying a colorful newspaper flyer advertising televisions. He takes off his reading glasses. "Come here, Garrett."

I step closer. Mr. Z stares up at me but says nothing. Our eyes meet and stay locked for several seconds.

"Most kids can't do that," he says.

My eyes remain on his, but I don't respond. He has not asked me a question.

Mr. Z puts the glasses back on, picks up some papers, and scans them. "You've been here for more than two months, Garrett. During that time you've spent a total of three weeks in TI. What have you learned so far?"

"That my parents are paying you a lot of money to turn me into a more obedient son, sir."

He lowers the papers and looks over the glasses at me with a slightly amused smirk. "You're a fast learner, Garrett. But that won't help you get out of here. You won't be able to fool us or convince us you're ready to go before you really are. Some of your fellow students foolishly cling to the notion that they can fake it. You know who they are because they're the ones who've been here the longest. Instead of learning from their mistakes, they just keep making the same ones. And the biggest mistake you can make here, Garrett, is thinking you can outsmart us. You may never have seen us before, but we've seen hundreds and hundreds of kids like you. I've been in this business for eleven years, and believe me, I've seen it all. We'll know when you're ready. And you will not leave a second before that."

The room becomes quiet.

"Any questions?" Mr. Z asks.

"No, sir."

He makes a tent of his stubby fingers and studies me. "I have a feeling there's a lot going on inside that brain, Garrett. A lot of mental energy being expended trying to find a loophole or some weakness you can exploit in order to get out of here. Rather than waste your time trying to think of ways to get around what you're supposed to be doing, why not spend that time and energy trying to understand why you were sent here and how you can change?"

Silence.

"Keep in mind, Garrett, that Lake Harmony is not an end. It's a means. A way of getting you back on track and headed in the right direction. Many of our graduates go on to two- and four-year colleges. Clearly, your parents have the ability to provide you with a wonderful education. Why waste your time and their money here when you could be enjoying life somewhere else?"

That reminds me of something. "Sir, may I ask a question that is in no way meant to be disrespectful?"

"Yes, Garrett, go ahead."

"Financially speaking, isn't it in your interest to keep us here as long as you can?"

Mr. Z smiles. "We couldn't have stayed in business all this time if we did that. Parents send their children here because we deliver results. That's our reputation, Garrett." He points at the old green file cabinets. "Inside some of those cabinets are letters of thanks from grateful parents who'd thought they'd lost their kids for good, sent them here out of absolute desperation, and then got back the kids they'd prayed for. You know what we do here, Garrett? We save lives. We're the last stop on the road to self-destruction, and we turn kids around and point them toward salvation. That's why I do what I do, Garrett. And as long as I keep doing that, there will always be parents who'll want to send their troubled children to me."

"Even if you have to beat them into submission, sir?"

Mr. Z's face goes stony. "That concludes our meeting, Garrett."

"One last question, sir?"

"What?" Mr. Z snaps, his voice oozing impatient displeasure.

"Sir, does every kid meet with you like this?"

Mr. Z draws a long breath in through his nose. "No, Garrett, they don't."

"Then why me, sir?"

Mr. Z gazes at me with an expression that's hard to read. "You can go."

The taped lectures that blare over the loudspeakers at mealtime are called RLs, which stands for Right Living. Just another example of Lake Harmony's conviction that before we came here we excelled in wrong living. Tonight's dinner lecture, broadcast at eardrum-bursting decibels, extols the merits of sleep: "Sufficient sleep positively affects our health and well-being and plays a key role in preventing disease and injury, promoting stability of mood and the ability to learn."

The only thing worse than these tapes is the food they serve while we listen to them. Greasy, fatty, and monotonous. Gray hamburgers, soggy French fries, watery spaghetti, slightly rancid-smelling tuna fish.

Given how foul the food is, hot dogs are a Lake Harmony favorite. For tonight's meal we each get two franks in buns and a fist-sized glob of mealy brown baked beans. What a feast!

"You bitch!" Tempers flare in the Courtesy family, where a tall blonde lunges across the table at another female. "Mothers," "fathers," and "chaperones" swarm over the two girls, pulling them apart.

Suddenly I feel a sharp poke in my ribs from the kid sitting next to me. It's David Zitface. He dips his pimply forehead in Adam's direction. I look across the table, where Adam meets my gaze and then looks down at the dogs on my plate.

He must be joking—or crazy—if he thinks I'm going to give him my hot dogs. If he wants part of my dinner, he can wait until a night when they're serving creamed chicken. Under the booming RL and the continued shouting at the Courtesy family table, Adam bares his lizard teeth menacingly. I ignore him. After a moment he turns his attention to Pauly, whose hot dogs sit untouched on his plate. Like a drop of food coloring in water, the red rash has spread and become diluted over his body.

"Ahem." Adam clears his throat. Pauly gazes up for a moment and shrugs as if he already knows what Adam wants. He wearily glances around to make sure

Joe and the chaperones aren't watching, then slides his plate toward Adam, who quickly picks off both dogs.

At the end of the meal, the glob of beans on Pauly's plate remains untouched. He hasn't eaten a thing.

After dinner we clear the tables and move on to Reflections, when we're supposed to write down our thoughts and what we learned from the RLs that day. (Level Fives and Sixes sometimes get to watch nonviolent PG movies and eat snacks like popcorn and potato chips in a special room off-limits to everyone else.) Once every two weeks we can write a letter to our parents (but nowhere else, and to no one else, including Sabrina). The RL is turned off, and we are given fat, bendable rubber markers. Pencils and pens are considered potential weapons.

There's no point in writing anything critical about Lake Harmony, because the chaperones read the letters and tear up any that disparage this wonderful institution. Up till now I haven't felt like writing. Wouldn't sending my parents a letter be doing them a favor? Letting them know I'm okay? And why should I do that? Why should I do anything that might make them feel good about sending me here? But for some reason today that feels dumb. What's the point? They know where I am. They may not hear from me, but that doesn't mean they don't call Mr. Z a few times a week to see how I'm "progressing."

Besides, can they really be serious about "rewiring" me? I'm sure they've heard that it's supposed to take a minimum of six to eight months. More likely a year to a year and a half. And in stubborn cases two years or more.

Two years? No way. I can't believe they'd send me away for that long. They're just trying to scare me. I can even remember the moment when they probably decided to do it. One morning I came home from Sabrina's and found them waiting for me in the living room. They were in their business clothes, my father wearing a white shirt, red tie, and blue suspenders with little sailboats on them, my mother in a coal-gray suit.

"You're going to be late for work," I said, glancing at my watch. Most mornings they were in their offices by seven A.M.

"This has got to stop," said my mother. She was talking about Sabrina.

"I'm home in time to go to school," I said. "What's the problem?"

"The problem is that it is inappropriate for you to be seeing a woman who is eight years older than you and your teacher," my mother said.

"She's not my teacher anymore," I reminded her. "You took care of that." After my mother found out about Sabrina and me, she complained to the school and got Sabrina fired. She even threatened to go to the police, but I knew she wouldn't.

"You're still seeing her," my father said.

"So?" I said.

"You are disobedient and uncooperative and out of control," my mother said. "You don't listen to us. You come and go as you please. You act as if you live here by yourself."

"Look, the one thing you've told me over and over is that you want me to go to an Ivy League college," I said. "I've got great grades, and high PSATs, and next year I'll start taking AP courses. I'm doing exactly what you want."

"You didn't go out for any sports," my mother said.

"I'm not athletic," I shot back.

"You don't do any extracurricular activities," she said.

"They're boring," I argued. "Look, let's be honest. There's nothing wrong with my life. You just don't like it, okay? I don't play the sports you want me to play. I didn't go to the camp you wanted me to go to. I'm not dating the kind of girl you want me to date. I don't like your friends, and I don't like your friends' kids. In other words, I don't fit into the life you imagined for me. But there's no law that says I have to."

"You've taken money from us," she said.

"You cut off my allowance," I said. "What was I supposed to do?"

"That doesn't make it right," said my father.

"Okay, so a couple of times I took forty, maybe fifty dollars," I admitted. "Most of my friends get double that a week in allowance. You guys are millionaires. Mom pays four hundred dollars to get her hair done. Your shirts cost two hundred and fifty. I'm amazed you even noticed the money was missing."

"What about this?" My father placed a small brass pipe on the coffee table. He must have found it in my room.

"Well, congratulations," I scoffed. "You just figured out that I'm one of the seventy percent of all teenagers who've tried pot."

My father cleared his throat. "I think what your mother and I are worried about is, if this is where you are at age fifteen, where will you be at age eighteen?"

"In college, just where you want me to be," I answered.

"It's not even about where he'll be at eighteen," my mother snapped at my father. "It's about where he is right now. He must end this relationship. It is simply unacceptable."

"Why?" I asked. "Because you're embarrassed by it? Because you can't stand the idea that your friends may be whispering behind your back? Because it's an affront to our family's high moral standards and lofty social status?"

"That's uncalled for," my father said calmly but firmly. "Your mother and I have worked very hard to get where we are."

"Well, good for you, but where you are isn't where I want to be. Now excuse me while I get ready for school." I left the room, banging the door hard behind me.

There were kids at the Governor's School who ditched way more than I did. Kids who smoked weed every morning before breakfast and did mushrooms every weekend. Guys who got their kicks breaking car windows. Girls who'd hook up with anyone who asked. Their parents didn't send them away. I went to school as much as I needed to maintain a 3.8 average. Maybe

I smoked once in a while with my friends, but mostly on weekends. The only thing I ever broke was curfew. *I don't deserve this.*

But at the same time, I can imagine how it happened. My mother is pathological about people whispering behind her back. She can't stand it. And she's in the business of damage control.

For the first time since I got here, I pick up the marker and begin to write a letter home. The words gush out, and for a few brief moments I almost forget where I am. That is, until Joe comes by and grabs the paper off my desk.

"Well, well," he announces loudly for the benefit of everyone, "look who finally decided to share his thoughts with us."

At the tables around me, kids look up, eager to listen. In that sudden wrenching moment, I realize I've made a terrible mistake. Joe gleefully clears his throat and begins reading:

"'Dear Mom and Dad, I guess you've been wondering when you'd hear from me. And you probably know why I haven't written. I still can't believe you sent me here. Both of you were in love once (at least I assume you were). Were you ever punished for that? Sent away for that?

"'Let's be honest. You're just embarrassed by me. I've made you look bad in front of your friends and business associates. That's why you sent me away. To show everyone that you know how to take charge and correct a bad situation. The same way a company always finds a scapegoat to blame when it's been caught breaking the law.

"'The trouble is, I'm not one of your clients. I'm your son. And if you think I'm going to thank you someday for sending me to this prison camp and "straightening me out," you're even more deluded than I thought.'"

With smug smiles on their faces most of the residents clearly enjoy the humiliation I'm feeling. But not all. I look up and into the sunken, darkly ringed eyes of Sarah. Our gazes connect. It's strange, because we've never spoken to each other, and yet somehow hers are the eyes I seek out more and more.

Meanwhile, Joe continues reading my letter:

"'One of the hardest things about this whole experience just may be how little faith you've shown in my ability to make the right decision. If you think you've taught me a lesson by sending me here, you're right. But it may not be the lesson you were hoping for. Anyway, I'm surviving, but I hope your medical insurance is all paid up, if you know what I mean.

I stare down at the table. My face feels like it's on fire, and all I can think about is ripping that letter out of Joe's grip while I land a solid right hook to his jaw. But that's exactly what they expect at Lake Harmony, isn't it? It would simply confirm what they already believe—that we've been sent here because we're violent and rebellious. Forget the inhuman treatment. Forget the endless humiliations. To prove we are good sons and daughters we must be willing to accept the abuse. After all, we deserve it, don't we?

"Almost two and a half months, Garrett," Joe says as he slowly tears up the letter, "and you haven't learned squat. So what's it going to be? You want to spend the next two years here like Sarah and still be a Level One? No hope of getting out until you turn eighteen? Or are you gonna realize that the only way out is to admit that you've been stupid and ignorant, but that you can change? You can learn from your mistakes. You can go back and have a life by listening to your parents. By appreciating and obeying them. By coming home at night and going to school and staying away from drugs *and* Sabrina. It's that easy, Garrett. A whole lot easier than spending the next two years here."

Pieces of the letter flutter to the floor. Joe is right about learning from my mistakes. I've just made one I will never make again.

Shut Down. Ron and Jon stand guard while we wash and use the bathroom. I'm brushing my teeth when David Zitface and Unibrow Robert come in and start to wash at the sinks on either side of me.

Zitface isn't a big kid, but he has a lean, rangy build. When Joe orders him to do push-ups, he completes them with relish, straight-backed, arms pumping like pistons, clearly proud that he can knock off twenty-five without breaking a sweat. He strikes me as a simple sort who sees everything in black and white, easily settled with fists. Unibrow, on the other hand, seems more ominous, more likely to do something unexpectedly nasty.

I bend down to get a mouthful of water. When I straighten back up, I feel something sharp poke into my back.

In the mirror I see Adam's face behind my left

shoulder. The toothbrush shiv in my back pricks my skin, and I stiffen in pain.

"You don't frickin' get it." Adam bares his little yellow teeth like some kind of large, meat-eating lizard.

There's no point in answering. The shiv goes deeper, and an involuntary gasp leaps from the back of my throat.

"I'm gonna tell you one more time," Adam says. "You do what I say, when I say it. I want your food, you give it to me. I tell you to stay away from Pauly, you do it. You may think Joe's in charge here, but I'm the one who runs this family."

A searing pain cuts across my lower back as Adam rakes my skin with the shiv. Then he, Zitface, and Unibrow march out of the bathroom. I slide my hand under my shirt and along the cut. When I look at my fingers again, they are red and sticky with blood.

ELEVEN

"Escape from Lake Harmony is not possible."

Written communication between residents is prohibited. The fat rubber markers used for writing are collected and counted at the end of study or Reflections. If one is missing, we go into lockdown mode, sitting in the food hall until the lost marker is found. No one leaves for any reason until all markers are accounted for. Apparently, here at Lake Harmony the pen is considered as mighty as the sword.

But there are ways to get around the rules. Out in the parking lot I found the nub of a pencil. That night after Shut Down I made a small hole in the seam of my pillow and hid the pencil like some kind of valuable jewel. Two days later I found the white wrapper from a roll of toilet paper. Yesterday at lunch I caught Sarah's eye, then wedged a note under the table where the leg met the tabletop. All she had to do was slide her hand under the edge of the table as she passed and she would find it.

why did you slash yourself?

After two and a half years there, she must have found a pen. At dinner I found her answer in the same spot where I'd left my note.

I'm going crazy here.

Today at breakfast I left another note.

But why hurt yourself?

At lunch she left another for me.

Who are you, my shrink?

I'm trying to help.

Don't waste your time.

In the morning we sit on our mattresses and bend over to tie the boots we run in. Pauly dips his head close to mine and whispers: "If we can get to Canada, we'll be safe."

He knows the penalty for talking. Ron and Jon are always hovering nearby, eager to earn points by informing on us. Pauly is risking a visit to TI. Or at the very least another round of push-ups, sit-ups, and squat thrusts.

"They can't get us there."

"Why tell me?" I whisper back.

"You're my only hope."

We're led outside by Mr. Sparks. At six-thirty A.M. the air is cool and heavy with mist. A dozen yards from us a male lies curled up and asleep on the ground, his ankle chained to a metal stake. His hair is wet with dew, and it's obvious he's been outside all night. Three months ago this sight would have been shocking. Now it's merely routine.

When we run, we're supposed to stay evenly spaced, far enough apart that we can't speak to each other. But that rarely happens, especially when Mr. Sparks accompanies us. He likes the exercise and doesn't seem to care whether we bunch up or not.

Halfway through the run someone grunts behind me, "Garrett, wait up!" Without turning I know it's Pauly. Part of me wants to tell him to go away and leave me alone because I don't want to get into trouble. But another part of me feels bad for the kid. I look around. Ron, Jon, and Mr. Sparks are nowhere to be seen. I slow down and let Pauly catch up. His face is red and glistening with sweat, and his polo shirt is covered with dark sweat stains.

"So what do you think?" he asks—half pant, half whisper—as we run.

"I don't know," I answer.

"It can't be that far," Pauly says.

I guess I believe him. "How?"

"I've got a plan. You, me, and Sarah."

● ● ●

Each morning and afternoon we have two-hour study periods. We sit in carrels and work at ancient Dells on programs that remind me of the workbooks we used in grade school. We go at our own pace, reading material on the computer and typing in answers at the end of each chapter, the silence broken only by the insect scamper of fingers on keyboards.

The reason why there are no actual classes is obvious: Real teachers cost more than "chaperones," and with so many kids going in and out of TI and other punishments, it would be impossible for everyone to stay on the same page. So we work by ourselves. If we run into a problem while on the computer, we place a small red flag on the top edge of the carrel and wait for a chaperone to appear.

Mr. Sparks comes over. "How can I help you, Garrett?"

I point at an equation on my computer screen: $f(x) = \sqrt{x-3}$.

"It says I can't have a negative value under the radical, so the value of x can be anything from three to infinity," I tell him. "But doesn't there have to be an actual upper limit? I mean, infinity can't be an actual value, can it, sir?"

Mr. Sparks leans down so his lips are close to my ear. "What the heck is that, Garrett?"

"Calculus, sir."

He grins. "Listen, my friend, guys in here usually have trouble with their multiplication tables. I don't have a clue what you're talking about."

"Oh well, thanks anyway, sir. I'll figure it out."

I expect Mr. Sparks to go back to his seat, but he stays close. "Man, what are you doing here?" he whispers.

It's been a week since I last saw Sarah. She hasn't been at meals or in Circle, so it's a pretty sure bet she's in TI. Then one morning she's back, looking even paler and more haggard than before. At lunch, while an RL on the empowering benefits of positive thought blasts out of the overhead speakers, she catches my eye. When Joe turns his back, I feel under the table and find a note:

Sorry I was such a bitch.

At dinner I write back.

It's okay. Like you said, you've been here a long time.

The following morning she writes:

Do you think Pauly's joke is funny?

It's code, in case our notes are found.

Not sure. What do you think?

I like it. Wish you did too.

"Tell us about Sabrina," Joe orders in Circle.

I feel myself grow tense. There's something sadistic in his ability to zero in on our most sensitive issues.

Of course the whole idea is to push our buttons, but Joe truly appears to relish it. I glance at Sarah, who is sitting next to Pauly across from me, but her return gaze is expressionless. Is she angry that I'm not more enthusiastic about Pauly's plan?

"Like what, sir?" I ask, trying to keep my voice steady.

"What do you think she's doing right now?"

"I don't know, sir."

"But you wonder, right? It's been three months since you saw her. A long time. She has no idea why you disappeared or where you are. No idea if she'll ever see you again. Chances are she's hurt and angry. Wouldn't you be if the person you loved suddenly vanished? She's probably wondering, if you love her so much, why haven't you called? She has to suspect that whatever's happened, you don't care enough to get in touch. Or maybe I've got it all backward. Maybe *she's* the one who doesn't care anymore. Maybe she's already found someone new."

These enticements to speculate are a common feature of Circle. They're an invitation to self-doubt and a call for the others to hurl abuse. The staff at Lake Harmony are a model of energy conservation. Why should they exert themselves beating you up physically or mentally when the residents are so eager to do it for them?

David Zitface is the first to pounce. "Definitely. I've known sluts like her. You know what they say: 'Out of sight, out of mind.' By now she's got to be with someone new."

"Someone old enough to drive," chimes in Chubby Girl, whose name is Rachel.

"She's probably relieved you're gone," adds Unibrow Robert. "Like, what was she doing with a kid like you anyway?"

I wonder what they'd say if they knew that the guy Sabrina had dated before me was verbally abusive and controlling. Or that she tried to break up with me twice, but both times we got back together. It was like we couldn't help ourselves.

"What are you thinking, Garrett?" Joe asks.

"I'm not sure I agree, sir."

"Then what do you think she's doing?"

"I don't know, sir."

Joe gives me a withering look as if he's getting fed up and impatient. "This is bull, smart guy. I want to hear something honest. I want to hear something private and personal right now, or you're going to TI."

When I don't answer right away, Joe stands up and starts toward the intercom next to the door. He's going to call a chaperone and have me taken to TI. Suddenly Sarah catches my eye and gives me an alarmed look.

"I worry, sir," I hear myself blurt.

Joe turns and stares expectantly at me.

I feel a catch in my throat. "I . . . I don't know what she's doing, sir. And that scares me."

Joe moves slowly back toward his chair, a nasty little smile on his lips. "She could be sleeping with your best friend. Or any of a hundred other guys."

An invisible weight presses down on my shoulders.

It's all about stripping you bare, leaving you defenseless and powerless.

"You're a frickin' fool if you think she's waiting for you," adds David Zitface.

"Definitely," Unibrow Robert agrees.

"And the longer you're gone, the more unlikely it is that she'll still be waiting when you come home," says Joe.

I nod. These thoughts have crossed my mind.

"So doesn't it feel pretty stupid that she's the reason you're here?" Joe asks.

But she's not the reason. My parents are.

"Well?" Joe wants a response.

"I guess, sir."

"You *guess*? You better do more than guess. You better agree. Your parents sent you here because they know what's best for you. When are you going to figure that out?"

It's pointless to answer.

No sign of Pauly. He's either in TI or the infirmary. I find another note from Sarah:

It must be hard not knowing.

what's hard is knowing that if it weren't
for my parents, we'd still be together.

*Doesn't it make sense to think about
what Pauly said?*

I don't see how it's possible. Escape from Lake Harmony?

Go to Canada? Then what? Forget it. There's got to be a better way out of this place.

Everyone is moody here. Students are happy when they earn points or rise to the next level. Losing points or getting kicked down a level is a descent into gloom. Sarah is moodier than most, with higher highs and lower lows. But ever since she chopped off her hair and slashed herself, there have been fewer highs, and the lows seem deeper and darker. The zombies like Ron and Jon walk around in a fog, but you sense they have hope. Somewhere in their rewired skulls they know they're getting out of here soon. But there are days now when Sarah subsists under a cloud of doom and hopelessness. Like Pauly's, her skin is pasty, and she's getting thinner. The bandages are off her arms, the skin streaked with long, thin, pink scars and dotted with yellowish-black bruises.

"Finish your food," her "mother" orders at lunch. The sloppy joe on Sarah's plate lies untouched.

"Put me up against a wall and shoot me," Sarah mutters, chin propped in her hand as if she doesn't have the will to hold her head up.

If any other student were that impudent, he or she would be sent to TI immediately. But they've apparently decided to handle Sarah differently.

"You won't leave until you eat at least half of it," her "mother" says.

"See you in the morning," Sarah replies.

why don't they send you to TI?

I've been there too many times.
They know it won't work.

Don't your parents wonder why it's taking
so long?

They don't want me back until I'm
fixed.

"You've been here since you were fourteen," Joe tells Sarah in Circle. "In a year and a half you'll be eighteen, and you'll be able to walk out no matter what your parents say. But by then you'll have been here for four years. Almost a quarter of your life wasted."

"So you think Lake Harmony's a waste?" Sarah replies smartly. Today she's in one of her rare spunky moods. But even when she's feeling good, it's obvious she no longer cares what they do to her.

Joe's nostrils flare for an instant. He's not used to such insolence. "It's not a waste for anyone else, but it is for you."

Sarah shrugs as if she doesn't care. Her skin is so pale, it's almost translucent, and her arms are bony. She reminds me of a story I once heard about a kid who held his breath until he fainted. Sarah will not give in to them, but that doesn't mean she won't break.

"You're a selfish, good-for-nothing, pathetic loser." We're in Circle, and Joe is ripping into a new girl named Megan. It's August, and I've been here for four months. Megan is solidly built and stocky with close-cropped blond hair and a permanent frown. Her ears, eyebrows, and lips have the telltale pinholes of piercings, and a black barbed-wire tattoo encircles her neck.

"You're so damn self-centered, you couldn't see how you were destroying your family with your drugs and lying and stealing," Joe says.

Pauly's rash has flared up again, and his neck and hands are covered with angry reddish splotches. By the yearning way he looks at me, I can tell that he wants to talk.

"Your mother has a full-time job and three young kids to take care of." Joe continues his tongue-lashing of Megan. "Instead of helping, you gave her every bit of grief you could. And why? Because your dad ran off with another woman?"

Maybe because she's a girl, no one is prepared when Megan rockets out of her chair and drives her head and shoulders into Joe's stomach like a linebacker. Joe gets slammed backward, and we hear the gruesome *thunk* as his head smacks against the wall. For an instant there's silence, as Joe collapses in an unconscious heap on the floor. No one can believe what just happened. Even Megan looks stunned at what she's done. Then she bolts out the door.

Alarms start to blare in the hall. Ron, who has recently been elevated to Level Six, races out to find help. Adam saunters to the front of the room and looks down at Joe, who is sprawled on the floor, unconscious, his arms and legs twisted in odd directions. Next Adam glances out into the hall, then motions to David Zitface and Unibrow Robert. The three of them slip out and vanish. I feel a hand on my shoulder. It's Pauly. He motions me toward the back of the room where Sarah is sitting.

I hesitate. This whole situation feels unreal. Joe out cold on the floor while the kids sit in their chairs, uncertain of what to do. There's the impulse to go get help, but why? Joe has caused me nothing but pain and anguish.

"Come on," Pauly hisses urgently, and tugs at my arm.

I follow him, and we turn our chairs into a small huddle so the other kids can't hear us under the jangling alarms. They sit in their seats watching us and waiting for someone to tell them what to do.

"It's gotta be soon," Pauly says in a hushed, rushed whisper. There's no way to know how much time we'll have before Joe wakes up or help comes. Sarah looks at me with dull, pleading eyes. Over the past few weeks it's seemed as if the life has slowly been drained out of them.

"The days are getting shorter," Pauly says. "In another couple of months it'll be too cold to go. Then we'll be stuck here all winter."

He and Sarah keep shooting me sideways glances, but I don't want to be in the position of saying yes or no.

"Maybe you should wait till spring," I suggest.

Sarah shakes her head slowly. "Mud season." Her voice sounds defeated, as if she senses my reluctance. "Cold, wet, and muddy." She knows, of course, because she's already been here for two springs.

Shouts and slapping footsteps come from the hall.

The alarm continues to clang. I glance at the front of the room, where Joe is still sprawled like a broken doll. It goes against my nature to sit there and do nothing, but I have to remind myself that there is nothing natural about being imprisoned at Lake Harmony.

"Sarah and I aren't going to make it through another winter," Pauly whispers.

Do they want me because they need someone strong and they're gambling that I'll be trustworthy?

I have to be honest with them. "I don't know."

Both Pauly and Sarah drop their heads in disappointment. The door opens and the troll rushes in, followed by Adam and his posse, who obviously think they're scoring major brownie points by coming to Joe's rescue. The troll slides his hands under Joe's armpits and drags him out of the room. Outside there are shouts and the sounds of feet slapping and a scuffle. Adam's eyes briefly go to Pauly, Sarah, and me; then he and his boys head back out to see what's going on.

"We're gonna start a fire," Pauly whispers desperately, as if to convince me that he has a plan.

I give him a dubious look.

"I'm serious," he insists.

"You mean, like in a wastepaper basket?" I ask.

"No, a *real* fire," Pauly says. "Sarah and I have been collecting stuff. We've got matches, a couple of bottles of nail-polish remover, some spray paint, and a bottle of alcohol from the infirmary. The rags won't be a problem. Everyone will have to evacuate. The fire department will have to come. In the confusion we sneak out."

"You set a real fire, and someone could die," I tell him.

"Another winter here and I'm dead anyway," Pauly says. He means it. Sarah nods in agreement.

Mr. Sparks enters the room. His clothes are askew, and he looks flustered as he tucks in his shirt. There's a long, reddish scratch on his arm and a smaller one under his left eye. "Everyone up. Back to quarters until further notice."

A female chaperone takes Sarah and the other girls back to the female wing. Mr. Sparks marches us males toward our dorm. We turn a corner, and lying on the floor is something that looks like a giant brown caterpillar with silver stripes. It's Megan, wrapped in a blanket that's been duct-taped closed like a full-body straight jacket. Duct tape covers her mouth as well. Her eyes are swollen shut, and her face is streaked with drying blood.

TWELVE

"You cannot initiate a visit to the infirmary."

It's a desperate plan. A thousand things could go wrong. I know they want and need me to join in, but I can't see taking that risk. The odds are way against them, but I'm worried just the same that they'll try it without me.

I leave Sarah a note:

Do you really think Pauly's joke is funny?

At the next meal she leaves her answer:

I'm not sure I care.

She's so up and down. But in a way the answer is reassuring. At least she's not gung ho to torch the place.

Two days later she leaves another note:

3 PM—Infirmary

Around two forty-five I'm in my carrel, studying chemistry on the computer, which makes no sense considering there are no labs for experiments. I prop my elbows on the desk, press my fingers against my temples, and close my eyes.

"What's up, Garrett?" Mr. Sparks comes over.

"Headache, sir."

He studies me. Kids are always making up excuses to go to the infirmary. Some want to get out of whatever job they're doing. Some are tired and want to rest. Some are just so desperate for a pill they'll settle for Tylenol. There have been times when I could have gone, like when I had that nosebleed with Joe, but I've purposefully resisted. I'm not even sure I knew why. It's almost as if instinctually I understood that I had to save them for when I really needed them.

"What do you want to do?" Mr. Sparks asks.

"Nothing, sir. It'll go away."

He accepts that answer and goes back to his chair. I pretend to look at the computer screen. Five minutes pass. Mr. Sparks returns. "You haven't touched the keyboard."

I fake a wince. "Give me a minute, sir. I'll get going."

"Yeah, right," Mr. Sparks says. "Ron, take Garrett to the infirmary."

Level Six automaton Ron pops out of his carrel

like a jack-in-the-box and accompanies me out of the room. I can't help thinking back to the night Harry and Rebecca first drove me here, and the way Harry lectured Rebecca when he thought I was trying to manipulate her. I may not have known much about manipulation then, but I've learned plenty about it since.

Out in the yard we cross the grass toward the infirmary. The breeze is dry and fresh, and it feels like fall is coming. A few leaves have begun to turn yellow. The Faith family of females is lined up in the yard doing jumping jacks, led by their "mother," who calls them sluts and whores. I can't believe I've been here for almost five months. It's like something out of Kafka. Instead of waking up as a giant cockroach, I've woken up in a penal colony.

The infirmary reminds me of the nurse's office at my old school, except that here the odor of stale cigarette smoke hangs in the air. There's a cot. A desk where the nurse sits. A curtain someone can get undressed behind. Oddly, an old metal safe. Sarah is lying on the cot. I frown at her. She mouths the word "cramps."

A toilet flushes somewhere behind the curtain, and a gray-haired guy comes out zipping up a pair of faded jeans. He's wearing an orange, yellow, and green tie-dyed T-shirt with a pack of cigarettes in the pocket, and his gray beard is braided. He has a gold earring, and tattoos on both arms. I assume he's a workman, so I'm caught by surprise when he sits down at the desk and gestures for me to sit in the chair beside it.

"Name?" he asks.

"Garrett Durrell, sir ... Uh ... forgive me for asking this, sir, but are you really the nurse here?"

He raises his head and gives me an amused look. "What? You never saw a male nurse before?"

"Not one who looked like an outlaw biker, sir."

"Ha-ha!" He slaps his hand against the desk. "That's good! If this place wants me to look like a frickin' nurse, they can pay me a nurse's wage." He blinks as if he's just realized what he's said and the trouble it could mean for him, then adds, "Only, you didn't hear that from me, right?"

"I don't even know what you're talking about, sir."

"You sure?" He narrows one eye suspiciously.

"Scout's honor, sir."

"You ever a scout?"

"No way, sir."

He grins—revealing yellowed, nicotine-stained teeth—and offers his hand for a shake. We've formed a strange, nearly instant bond, as if our built-in BS detectors work on the same wavelength.

"My name's Ted," he says. "So what can I do for you, Garrett?"

"Sir, Mr. Sparks sent me here because I have a headache."

Ted opens a drawer, takes out a small electronic thermometer, and sticks it in my ear. "Your temperature's normal."

"I told Mr. Sparks it would probably go away, sir."

"Want some OxyContin?" Ted asks.

I hesitate uncertainly.

"It's the best thing for a headache," Ted says. "Take

care of it in no time. What do you say?"

"OxyContin is an addictive narcotic, sir. It's not the sort of thing you'd be handing out here."

Ted grins again. "Good for you, Garrett. You passed the test." He gives me a couple of Tylenol, then turns to Sarah. "How you doing?"

Sarah rolls her eyes.

"Glad I'm not a female," Ted mumbles. The phone rings and he picks it up. "Yeah? What? Ah, for God's sake. No, don't move her. Yeah, I'll be right there."

He hangs up. "I gotta go check on a kid who fell and hurt her neck. I'm only gonna be gone a minute, and I'm trusting you two not to get into any mischief, right?"

Sarah and I both nod.

"Don't bother looking for the good stuff while I'm gone, Garrett. It's all locked in the safe." He goes out and closes the door behind him. It's hard to believe this guy is Lake Harmony's nurse, except that he must come a lot cheaper than a real RN.

Suddenly Sarah and I are alone. It appears that she's lost even more weight. Her elbows and wrists are bony, and her face seems longer, but it's probably just thinner. Her skin has an odd, translucent quality, but her gaze is steady, and her blue eyes have an intensity I haven't seen in weeks. "You're never going to get out of here," she says in a determined but almost imperceptible whisper. "The problem is, by the time you figure that out, it'll be too late for Pauly and me."

I hang my head regretfully. I had a feeling she

was going to try again to get me to help her and Pauly escape. When I look up, her eyes are watery.

"My father is a Mormon elder and apostle," she whispers, and wipes a tear off her cheek. "Do you know what that is?"

"Someone pretty important in the Mormon church?" She nods.

"Couldn't you fake it?" I ask.

"I tried, but it's like this place. They know when you're BSing them. The problem is, unlike this place they're not set up to deal with subversives. They only know how to preach to the faithful. I'm here because they don't want me contaminating the flock."

"Can't you go live with a friend or someone?"

"My father won't allow it. Either I'm with him or I'm here. When you're that high up in the church, you can't be perceived as failing. And it's not just an image thing. He absolutely believes that I'm doomed if I don't join the fold. So I might as well be here, because I'm damned wherever I am."

"What about a relative?"

"Tried that. My mom's parents went to court to try to get guardianship and lost. Somehow my aunt found out where I was and actually came here to get me, but they wouldn't let her in."

I feel a pang. So she really is stuck here. How can this happen in a democracy that was allegedly founded on the idea of personal liberty, freedom of choice, and the rights of the individual?

Because until you turn eighteen you are not considered an individual.

And you have no rights.

It's insanity.

Once again, Sarah's eyes become teary. "You see how unfair it is?"

"Yes."

The next question hangs unvoiced in the air between us. How can I *not* help Pauly and her try to escape?

The office door opens and Ted comes in. "Anyone feeling any better?"

Sarah and I lock eyes. Hers are pleading. I look away.

"The headache's gone, sir," I tell him.

It's lunchtime, and Joe is back patrolling the tables. This is the first time I've seen him since Megan knocked him out, and except for the lump bulging from the back of his head, he seems the same as before. There's been no sign of Megan.

"Ahem." Adam clears his throat. Today he's decided to sit directly across from me. On the menu are small, leathery hamburgers on stale buns, and french fries. The fries glisten with grease, but for once they're well done and crispy. Around the table they're disappearing from plates a lot faster than the hamburgers.

"Ahem." Adam clears his throat again and nods at my plate. As if I'm going to give him the first tasty thing we've had to eat in weeks. I shoot him a look to let him know hell will freeze over before he gets one of my fries. He smiles back and reaches into his pocket. Out comes a familiar piece of torn white paper. It's one of the notes I wrote to Sarah. I have no idea how he got it.

Adam gestures again at my french fries, like he

wants to make a deal. I make a fist and bring it up under my chin. When Joe's back is turned and none of the chaperones are looking, I flip Adam the bird. His pasty face goes stony, eyes squinting and lizard teeth clenched. A moment later, when Joe passes, Adam holds up the note. "Sir? Look what I found."

Joe takes the note and studies it. "Someone here write this?"

Adam points at me.

"This yours, Garrett?" Joe asks.

"Sorry, sir?" I shake my head innocently.

"Keep an eye on them, Mr. Gold," Joe orders, and walks over to the shelf where our Reflections notebooks are stored. He opens mine and starts to compare the note to the handwriting inside. I watch as the corners of his mouth drop and the wrinkles in his forehead deepen. He closes my notebook and then opens another, and then another, trying to find a match. Finally he puts the notebooks back and shoves the note into his pocket.

Adam frowns. As if I'd tell him I wrote those notes with my left hand.

"I'd be dead if I wasn't here," Chubby Rachel says in Circle. You hear this a lot. Maybe it represents a turning point in the rewiring process. The point at which you acknowledge that everything you did before was wrong.

"How?" I ask, enjoying for the moment Level Two status, which allows me to speak without permission. It's ironic that all I had to do was what was expected of me—which I was doing anyway—to earn the points to reach Level Two while Joe was busy torturing some other new recruits.

"What?" Chubby Rachel doesn't seem to understand.

"How would you have died?" I ask.

"Uh . . . I don't know."

"Then how do you know?" I ask.

"She just knows, okay?" Adam says.

"What about you, Adam?" I ask, although I'm surprised that Joe hasn't told me to shut up.

"What about me?" Adam shoots back.

"Would you be dead by now too?"

Adam makes a face. It's so obvious that he thinks that line is a load of crap. But he knows better than to say so. "Yeah, sure."

"Let me guess," I go on. "You'd have gone out in a hail of bullets. A regular *Butch Cassidy and the Sundance Kid.*"

Adam crosses his arms and glowers. I glance around at the rest of the residents in Circle, but no one seems to get it. Sarah is gazing off at a blank wall, not even listening. Pauly is watching with nervous, jittery eyes, as if he's so scared someone will pick on him that he can't focus on anything else.

"You think you're smart 'cause you can quote from books," Adam spits.

"It was a movie, stupid," says Sarah. So she has been listening after all.

"Whatever." Adam shrugs.

"You know, they say knowledge is a dangerous thing," I go on. "It gives people ideas. One thing almost every dictator in history has had in common was trying to limit people's access to knowledge, to books, newspapers, free speech, any news from the outside world." I wonder if they realize I'm talking about Lake Harmony.

Adam glances at Joe, as if he's uncomfortable with the direction of the conversation and wants our "father" to come to his rescue. But Joe just stares at the floor. Adam looks back at me. "What's your point?"

"My point is that just because we're in here doesn't mean the outside world no longer exists," I tell him. "You seem to think that the only rules are Lake Harmony's, and that as long as you and your henchmen carry out secret missions for Joe, you're somehow protected. But what you don't understand is that that only works in here, not out there. You don't believe that crap about being dead if you were still out there. You think you'd be doing the same stuff you do in here and you'd get by. But what are you gonna do out there, Adam? Be a gangsta? A bodyguard for some rap star? You think you're such a tough guy, but you don't understand that it's only because they *let* you be a tough guy. Don't you see that you're just their puppet? They're using you and your posse to do the dirty work they're not allowed to do."

Amazingly, Adam stares at Joe as if he needs to know if this is true.

"You have to be kidding me, Adam," I tell him. "It never occurred to you that there was something strange going on when you and your goons could terrorize

Pauly in the bathroom and still not get turned in by Ron or Jon?"

Adam is still staring at Joe. In a way I'm as surprised as Adam is. I'd naturally assumed that he and Joe had an understanding.

"Adam, how long have you been here?" I ask. "A year? A year and a half?"

He doesn't answer. His eyes dart back and forth between me and Joe with a look of desperate uncertainty.

"You think you're ever gonna get out?" I ask. "You must be crazy. They *need* you here. You're their perfect enforcer. Their junior terrorist puppet. They don't even have to tell you what to do, because that sick brain of yours automatically seems to know."

Circle has gone silent. Most of the kids are looking at Joe, as if waiting to see what he'll say. But Sarah stares at me with eyes filled with dread and warning. Finally Joe lifts his head, a sinister smile on his lips. Suddenly I feel a chill.

"Always good to hear what's on your mind, Garrett," Joe says, his smile triumphant.

Adam sits back in his chair, crossing his arms and gloating. My extremities grow cold, and I feel myself withdraw. A poisonous cloud of regret settles around me. They set a trap and I walked into it with eyes wide open. *Bang!* In my mind a door slams shut. A key turns.

Sarah gives me a pained expression. Almost as if she's disappointed.

Joe nods slowly. "Guess you're not as smart as you thought, Garrett."

Guess not.

"Back to TI, smart guy."

THIRTEEN

"Prolonged periods of physical restraint may be necessary."

The concrete floor of TI feels colder than last time. Fall has arrived. I've lost count of how many days I've been here and how many times Ron and Jon have come in to twist my legs and arms and leave no visible marks or bruises. Every part of my body hurts.

In a bizarre way, the distraction of the pain is almost a relief from the worst torture of all—the hours alone with nothing to do but think. You begin to ask yourself what you could possibly do to get out of this damp, chilly room and off this cold, grimy floor. And that's when the inevitable thought arrives:

Was being with Sabrina worth this?

No! No! No! Don't think that! That's exactly what they want!

This is how the rewiring begins. If I'd been sent here for eating M&M's, wouldn't I be wondering right now if it was worth it? If it meant getting off this miserable floor and sleeping in a bed and seeing other humans, wouldn't I agree never to play video games again? If they keep me here long enough, I'll eventually agree to anything. Fill in the blank: "If you'll let me out of here, I swear I'll _____."

a) never use bad words again

b) stop picking my nose

c) dot the *i* and cross the *t*

d) listen to my parents

It makes me wonder how Sarah has been able to withstand it for as long as she has. It doesn't seem humanly possible. Pauly, too, in his own strange way. I can't imagine the inner strength it must take. I've been here five months. They've been here for years. If I were either of them, I probably would have given in a long time ago.

All you have to do is listen to your parents.

This is why Lake Harmony works. Because it has to. Sooner or later I will believe whatever they want me to believe.

"Are you ready to listen to your parents?" Ron demands, standing over me with one foot on my neck, pressing my face into the floor while Jon twists my right ankle.

"Yes, sir," I hear myself answer weakly.

"Liar!" Ron shouts.

"No, I mean it, sir. I swear."

"You'll say anything to get out of here."

True.

"How do we know you're not lying?" Jon asks.

"I'll prove it, sir," I blurt out in desperation.

"How?" asks Ron.

"Sir, you tell me."

The pressure on my face eases as Ron takes his foot off my neck. Jon lets go of my ankle. It's a relief to rub the grime off my sore cheek where it was flattened against the floor.

"I'll be back," Ron says.

His shoes head toward the door. It opens and closes. I don't know where he's gone, but for the first time in what seems like an eternity, I feel hope. The hope that I'll soon get out of TI.

A little while later the door opens. Two sets of shoes come in. One set belongs to Ron. The second set is Joe's.

"Ron says you've had a change of heart, Garrett."

"Yes, sir."

"Sit up."

I press my palms against the floor and slowly push myself up. Joe hands me a clipboard with a piece of lined paper and a fat rubber marker.

"Do I have to tell you what to do?" Joe asks.

"Write a letter to my parents, sir?"

"No, Garrett. Write a letter . . . to Sabrina."

Dear Sabrina,
You haven't heard from me because

my parents sent me away and I'm not allowed to contact anyone. The reason they did it was to give me time to think about the decisions I've made. As you know, my parents were against our relationship from the beginning. I disobeyed them to be with you. Now that I've had time to think, I can see why they felt the way they did. They've always wanted the best for me, and I understand why they think you and I are wrong together. I'm sorry, but I realize now that I made a mistake. I should have listened to my parents more carefully. Sincerely,

Garrett

Joe has left to do other things, so I fold the letter carefully and hand it to Jon, who immediately opens and reads it, then hands it to Ron to read. Meanwhile, I try to hide the discomfort I feel at these strangers reading something so personal.

"What do you think?" Jon asks Ron.

"Let me show it to Joe," Ron says and leaves.

The minutes pass, but at least I've accomplished something: I get to sit instead of lie facedown. Rarely has something so mundane felt so momentous. Like that first breath after being held underwater.

"See, getting with the program isn't so hard," Jon

suddenly says. "It's all about facing your mistakes, man. We've all made 'em, or we wouldn't be here. Joe and Mr. Z and all the rest of them are just trying to help us. It's a good thing my mom sent me here when she did, because—"

Otherwise you'd be dead by now?

"—I never would have made it. I'd have died for sure. And believe me, if I can make it, anyone can, 'cause I was one seriously messed-up jerk. I'm telling you, Garrett, you can do it. You gotta do it. Once you're here, there's no choice. And once you do it, you realize it's good for you, man. I'm telling you, this is the best thing that's ever happened to me."

The zeal of the newly converted . . .

The door opens and Joe comes in, followed by Ron. Joe holds up the letter, a knowing look on his face. "Nice try, smart guy. I mean, at first glance it's halfway convincing. This stuff about how you can see why your parents felt the way they did. Very clever till you read between the lines and realize that nowhere do you admit that what you did was wrong. And then that last sentence about how you should have listened more carefully to your parents? Right, so you would have known what they were planning."

Just as he did with the last letter I wrote, Joe holds this one out in front of him like a dirty diaper and slowly shreds it. I'm waiting for the order to lie on the floor again, when he says, "Get up."

The command catches me by surprise, and Joe sees it in my eyes. "What? You thought I was gonna make you stay here for another week? Nah, come on, what kind of guy do you think I am?"

I rise to my feet uncertainly. What's he up to?

"You did okay, Garrett," Joe goes on. "You wrote a letter. It ain't good enough, but it's a start. See how it works here, buddy? You play ball with us, we play ball with you. You let me know when you're ready to write another one."

"Come on, Garrett, pass it! Pass it!" Mr. Sparks shouts. We're playing soccer, and I'm dribbling the ball down the right side of the field deep in the opposing team's territory. Mr. Sparks is running parallel to me about fifty feet to my left. The only defender left between us and the goalie is Pauly, who's spent most of the game standing in the same spot. As Mr. Sparks and I come toward him, he catches my eye, jerks his head toward Mr. Sparks, and mouths the words "Pass it!"

Even though we only play about once a month, soccer is the preferred sport for lower-level residents at Lake Harmony because the field is big and keeps us spread far apart, thus discouraging conversations. Until a moment ago, I was actually having fun. It's a blue-sky, crisp fall day, too chilly to stand around without a jacket, but not bad as long as you keep running. Mr. Sparks loves soccer. He started out as the ref, but when Unibrow Robert grabbed his side and complained of a stitch, he eagerly took Robert's place and became a player, too.

I pass the ball to him, and he heads toward the goal. Now only Adam, the goalie, stands between him and a score. Meanwhile, beside me Pauly wastes no time.

"There's a circuit-breaker box in the hall outside our dorm," he whispers. "I'm pretty sure it's the master switch for the whole camp. We pass it every day. All we need to do is start a commotion, and I'll open it and pull the main breaker. Soon as the power goes off, the doors will automatically unlock and the alarms won't work."

There's a desperate determination in his voice. As if he truly believes that it's a life or death situation and this crazy plan is his only hope. From my look of doubt, he must know what I'm thinking.

"My father is Mr. Handyman," he explains. "He was always showing me this stuff, because 'real men' know how to fix things. Kind of ironic when you think about it."

"So you pull the breaker and all the lights go off. What stops them from turning the breaker back on?" I ask.

"Sarah's got a padlock. It came with her suitcase and she hid it when they weren't looking. It's probably not that strong, but it'll still take them a while in the dark to find a wrench or something to jimmy the lock and turn the electricity back on."

"And in the meantime?" I ask.

"We start the fire."

"Score!" Mr. Sparks shouts triumphantly after kicking the ball past Adam and into the goal. The chaperone runs back toward midfield with his arms raised.

Pauly doesn't miss a beat. "As soon as the power's off, kids will go crazy. With the alarms dead, they'll take off in every direction. It'll be total mayhem. Then when they open the gate to let the fire trucks in, we sneak out."

Knowing the little I know about Pauly, I wouldn't have thought him capable of coming up with such an audacious plan. As if he's read my thoughts, he points at his head. "What I lack in physical strength, I make up for here. Too bad my father could never figure that out."

"Come on, Garrett! Let's go!" Mr. Sparks shouts as the teams line up to start playing again.

I slowly turn away from Pauly.

"Last night was a full moon," he says in a frantic rush behind me. "That means in two weeks it'll be the new moon. The darkest night of the month. That's when we have to go."

FOURTEEN

"You will continue your educational studies in order to remain on grade level."

Crash! One day about a week later an incredibly heavy cardboard box smashes into the carrel where I'm studying, knocking me sideways against the wall and pinning me there. It's too big and heavy to get my arms around. I'm trapped with the smell of cardboard in my nose and dust in my eyes. The box weighs a ton. Most of it's on my left thigh, pinning it down on the chair painfully and cutting off the circulation. Even as my left foot begins to tingle from lack of blood, I have a feeling I'm lucky. Had the box knocked me over completely, I could have been crushed.

"Get it off him!" someone shouts. Sounds like the troll. I hear quick scuffling footsteps, then the dry slither of hands sliding over the cardboard as they try to get a grip.

"Easy!" the troll shouts. "Come on, lift!"

The box starts to rise, but someone loses his grip and the full weight of it thuds back down, once again crushing my leg painfully.

"For God's sake!" the troll yells.

Once again hands slide around the box and start to lift. I manage to get my fingertips under the bottom edge to help, but pinned the way I am it's hard to get any leverage.

"Careful!" the troll shouts. "Easy! Don't let it fall! It's a brand-new Sony!"

Accompanied by a small chorus of grunts and groans, the heavy box slowly eases off me. The pain in my leg subsides, and I can feel the blood start to flow back to my tingling foot.

"Careful! Careful!" the troll urges. "If this thing is broken, I'll have your hides."

The box slides away. Now that the pain in my leg is easing, I become aware of a deeper, pulsing ache from the side of my head to the top of my right shoulder— the part of my body that slammed against the wall when the box crashed down. The pain slowly creeps around my skull and becomes a pounding, brain-rattling headache of such intensity that it hurts to open my eyes and focus. But when I do, I see that it's Adam, David Zitface, and Unibrow Robert who've pulled the box off me.

Of course. They're the ones who dropped the box in the first place. I shouldn't be surprised, but sweet Jesus, I could have been killed. The burst of anger that surges through me tips my headache over the edge into blinding pain.

Meanwhile, the troll yells, "Stand back!" There's a ripping sound as he quickly opens the box. "Come on, help me."

Adam and his posse help the troll tear away the cardboard. The TV inside is big and bulky and encased in white Styrofoam. While they're preoccupied with concern for the Sony, Pauly takes the opportunity to sidle up.

"Adam did that on purpose," he whispers.

No kidding. I've started to tremble, partly because of how close I just came to being really hurt, partly in anger, and partly thanks to this debilitating headache. Were it not for the pain, I would beat Adam into a bloody pulp.

"He's not going to stop," Pauly whispers. "You stood up to him, and he can't stand that. Besides, as long as he does what Joe tells him to do, he thinks he can't get in trouble."

As if Adam senses what Pauly is saying, he looks up from the TV and arches an eyebrow disdainfully, clearly disappointed I wasn't more badly hurt.

"The new moon is in six days," Pauly whispers.

The door opens and Joe stalks in. "What the hell is going on?"

"Nothing, it's okay," the troll answers. "The boys were moving the new TV to the upper-level lounge, and it slipped and hit Garrett—" The troll falters and looks in my direction for the first time. "You okay, Garrett?"

I nod, but there's no mistaking the disapproval in Joe's eyes as he stares icily at Adam, who shrugs back innocently as if it really were an accident. But that's a crock and everyone knows it.

Joe turns his attention to Pauly and me. "Back to your carrels."

"Six days," Pauly hisses one last time, and turns away.

FIFTEEN

"You will be held accountable for your actions."

Parents can visit after six months. "Garrett's parents are coming tomorrow," Joe tells us at Shut Down. "You know what that means. Any infraction will be punished in the severest way possible. Any Level Four or higher will be busted all the way back down to Level One. Level Threes and below can expect a prolonged vacation in TI with weekly visits from Level Sixes. After the crap Megan pulled, the word from upstairs is we're cracking down extra hard. That means zero tolerance and maximum behavior modification. I wouldn't want to be the next kid who screws up."

That night I hardly sleep. How can I convince my

parents that sending me here was a huge mistake? I know they thought they were doing the right thing, but I'm certain they didn't know that this place is a penal colony where inmates have even fewer rights than murderers doing life without parole.

In the morning we wash, make our beds, and line up for the day's orders. Joe arrives, wearing a windbreaker and a baseball cap.

"Boots on," he barks. "We're running."

We pull on our boots and get back in line. Mr. Sparks arrives to lead the run, but as we leave the dorm, Joe shouts. "Garrett, step out!"

I stop and let the others pass. From outside comes the scent of smoke as if from a woodstove. Joe doesn't miss a trick. Seeing the way I pause to gaze through the open doorway, he catches the door just as it's closing.

"Want to step outside?" he asks, knowing that of course I do. Life inside is so oppressive and regimented that the outdoors has come to represent freedom, even if we are still watched most of the time.

Outside I take a deep breath of the cool morning air. It feels so fresh, so different from the staleness inside. A light mist hangs over the grounds and makes the yellow and red trees look slightly out of focus. From the distance comes the faintest sound of what I could swear is a fog horn. The cool air quickly seeps through my polo shirt, and I feel a chill as goose bumps rise on my arms. Joe zips up his jacket.

"Nice being outside, isn't it?" He goes into his buddy-buddy act once the others have trotted off into the mist.

"A little chilly, but yes, sir."

"Know how easy it would be to have this any time you wanted?"

The answer is obvious. It would be as easy as admitting that being with Sabrina was wrong, that disagreeing with my parents is wrong, that having a mind of my own is unacceptable.

"I asked you a question, Garrett," Joe says.

"Yes, sir, I know how easy it would be."

Sensing that he isn't going to get the answer he wants, Joe's face tightens and the convivial mood vanishes. "In accordance with Lake Harmony policy, I will be accompanying you and your parents during their visit today," he announces. "They have already been warned that you may try to tell them things about Lake Harmony that are untrue. They understand that the students here are skilled manipulators who know how to pull on their parents' heartstrings by telling them horror stories of beatings and abuse. I have some advice for you, Garrett: Don't try it."

From somewhere in the distance beyond the red and yellow trees comes that faint foghorn sound again. Across the field the other members of the Dignity family jog out of the mist single file. They've finished the first mile and have four more to go. Ron and Jon lead as usual. Adam, David, and Robert are toward the back. The last straggler, as always, is Pauly.

"Go ahead and join your family," Joe says. "Just remember. If you ever want to get out of here, you'll be careful about what you say today."

● ● ●

"Garrett Durrell to the office." The call comes after lunch. I'm in my carrel working on the computer. I've felt edgy all morning, but as I rise from my chair, I can feel my heart start to race and a light sweat dot my forehead. Weird to think I'm feeling this way about my parents, toward whom I've been nothing but royally pissed since they sent me here six months ago.

"Excuse me!" Mr. Sparks snaps.

I realize my mistake and quickly sit back down. I know I'm not supposed to speak, but just the same I say, "Sorry, sir."

There's just the hint of a smile on Mr. Sparks's lips as he says, "Don't let it happen again. Someone will come and get you."

I wait in my carrel until Ron shows up. "Let's go."

We head outside and across the grass to the administration building. The sun is higher now and has burned off the early-morning haze. The air is crisp and has that special fall clarity. The trees, the flagpole, everything seems to be in extra sharp focus. The memory of that foghorn flits briefly across my mind and vanishes again.

We enter the administration-building lobby. My father is standing with his back to me, speaking to Joe. Like me, he towers over our group "father." Dad is wearing an emerald-green crewneck sweater, khaki slacks, and brown loafers with tassels. All morning I've encountered unexpected emotions—nervousness, eagerness, anxiety—but none more surprising than what I feel at this instant: an intense impulse to cry.

What is this? Why the watery eyes? The answer

is instantaneous. I want him to get me out of here immediately. I want him to say he's made a terrible mistake and that he's come to take me home.

I'm glad his back is turned, as it gives me an extra moment to blink away the tears. Then he swivels, smiles when he sees me, and holds out his hand. "Garrett, how are you?"

Emotions well up inside me and threaten to erupt. I catch my breath and fight the sudden and intense yearning to blurt out how horrible this place is. How absolutely unbelievable it is that he and Mom sent me here. *What were you thinking? Did you have any idea what you were doing?*

Joe is standing slightly behind my father, and I can't miss the squeezed eyebrows and furrowed forehead warning me to stay in line. I muster every bit of self-control and shake my real father's hand. "Where's Mom?"

He gazes down at the floor. "She, uh, couldn't make it. Something last-minute came up. At work."

The disappointment I feel is palpable, but this is so typical that I can't believe it caught me by surprise. First time she can see me in six months and she can't make it because of work. But it was always that way. Dad would show up for the school play, the band performance, and the book fair. If Mom made it to school twice a year, it was a lot. Work always came first. The excuse she gave was that it was her company. It was up to her to make sure everything ran correctly. There was always something that had to be done.

"So, why don't we start by showing you where

Garrett lives," Joe says, eager to get things moving. He heads toward the door. It's one of those rare moments when his back is turned, and I reach out and grab a brochure from the stack on the table and slide it into my pocket. Later, while we're touring the food hall, I hide it in my Reflections notebook.

The visit goes just as Joe had hoped. My father gets the grand tour. Joe sticks to us like a nervous parent chaperoning his daughter's first date. I keep waiting for my father to ask if he can have a moment with me alone, but it never happens. I can only assume that Lake Harmony warned him ahead of time that it wouldn't be allowed.

Joe takes us through the gymnasium and the upper-level TV lounge, where the new flat-screen Sony sits in front of two dozen empty chairs, and crumpled snack bags fill the garbage. Despite having been at Lake Harmony for six months, this is the first time I've set foot in either of these places.

"As you can see, Mr. Durrell, we have a full range of athletic activities." Joe has a way of addressing my father while keeping his eyes on me, sending warning looks that if I say the wrong thing I will pay dearly.

"Yes," my father replies. "Very nice."

"You know what I was wondering, Dad," I say, realizing that in my father's presence I don't have to obey the rule of not speaking unless spoken to. I can feel Joe tense apprehensively. "How did you and Mom pick Lake Harmony in the first place?"

Joe relaxes. The question seems harmless.

"It took a lot of research," Dad answers. "We spoke

to other families. Even used a consultant. This was the place people kept mentioning. They have an excellent record of results. One thing you can't fake is word of mouth. That's how we knew this was the right place for you."

Joe smiles proudly.

"You know," my father continues, "Joe sent us the letter you wrote."

Huh? I don't know what he's talking about. "What letter?"

"The one you wrote to . . . that woman." Neither of my parents has ever been able to utter Sabrina's name out loud. But I still don't understand. I only wrote one letter, and Joe tore it up.

"That's a big step forward," my father goes on. "It shows how far you've come."

I glance quizzically at Joe, who gives me a knowing look. Now I get it. When Ron brought the letter to him, he made a copy to send to my parents. He and I knew it didn't represent all that much "progress," but it was good enough to fool my folks. After all, at the six-month mark my parents have shelled out twenty-four thousand dollars. Lake Harmony has to show something for all those Franklins.

The last stop is my "classroom," where Joe brags about the "quality" education we're receiving. The visit ends after about three hours. Suddenly it's time for my father to return to the airport and catch the last flight out.

As we walk across the parking lot to his rented car, Joe lags behind as if to give us some privacy, but not so far as to be out of earshot. My father puts his hand on my shoulder. "Look, Garrett, I know this isn't easy for you. You must be very angry with us. I just hope you understand that we did this because we love you and want the best for you. Try to take the long view. This is about your future. Getting there may be hard and unpleasant, but I truly believe that once you're there, you'll be glad."

"Once I'm where?" I ask.

"Where you should be," Dad says. "I mean, in terms of maturity."

"What's maturity?" I ask.

He frowns uncertainly. "Well, I guess it's having the judgment to know what's good for you and what isn't."

Dark, gloomy clouds begin to gather overhead. It looks like I'm going to stay at Lake Harmony until I become "mature." The definition of maturity being "seeing things the way my parents do." My father didn't come here to say that he and Mom realize they were wrong, or to apologize, or to take me home. He came here to make sure I still have two arms and two legs. And having found that to be the case, he is now on his way home believing his son is in good hands and "making progress." He will see me again in another six months. Or possibly sooner if I somehow miraculously become "mature."

We shake hands, and he gets into the rental car and drives away. As I watch the car roll through the tall metal gate, it completely knocks the wind out of me.

I feel like I've been blindsided. Sometimes you don't realize what dream or wish you've pinned your hopes on until that dream comes and goes. Once again, tears threaten to spill out of my eyes.

"Let's go," Joe says behind me.

I blink, then pretend to sneeze in order to wipe the tears away without him seeing. Joe silently escorts me from the parking lot. It's dinnertime, so I assume he's taking me back to the food hall.

"Not that way," Joe orders.

"Sorry, sir?"

Joe marches me to the small windowless room where I was brought when I first arrived. He closes the door and says, "Strip."

SIXTEEN

"You are required to participate in all physical activities."

I do as I'm told and stand naked and shivering while Joe searches my clothes and then me. Only then am I allowed to dress and proceed to the food hall.

Pauly and Sarah both stare when I enter. I have the oddest sensation that somehow Pauly got word to Sarah about the visit and they're watching to see how it went. An RL about good nutrition mixes with the crappy smell of cheap, overcooked food. Not that it matters. Eating is the last thing on my mind. Where there might have been an appetite, there is now a numb sensation. I'm stunned by what has just happened. How could my father drive away and leave me here?

The answer doesn't matter. What does matter is that now I know for certain that I'm trapped in this freakin' nightmare called Lake Harmony until I renounce my old self, espouse the program's belief system, display gratitude for my salvation, and demonstrate my deliverance by policing fellow students who resist.

Suddenly I'm hit by a new sensation. My bladder feels like it's going to explode. I realize I never went this morning. I stop and raise one finger.

Ron accompanies me out into the hallway and toward the closest bathroom. As we round a corner, I glimpse Joe and Adam outside the Circle room. Joe's lips are inches from Adam's ear. As he speaks, Adam nods. Neither notices me.

I do my business and return to the food hall. Carrying a tray, I sit down, aware that the other members of my "family" are giving me curious looks. Everyone knows about my visit today. With the RL blaring in my ears— *"The mineral calcium not only builds and strengthens bones and teeth, it also maintains normal heartbeat and regulates blood pressure"*—I stare down at dinner. Tonight is the once-weekly event called "train crash," when they more or less mix all the week's leftovers together in tomato sauce. Too bad my father didn't stay long enough to sample this marvelous culinary achievement.

Adam arrives late with his tray and sits down. My "family" eats while the RL goes on: *A diet rich in fruits, vegetables, nuts, yogurt, legumes, eggs, vegetable oils, whole grains, tea, and water results in less skin wrinkling than a diet composed primarily of red meat, whole milk, butter, sugared products, and potatoes."* I can only assume that no one is listening. Otherwise they would realize the hypocrisy of what they're hearing. Hardly a meal is served here without butter, sugared products, and potatoes. I'm surrounded by dozens of pasty-faced, pimply kids.

No one cares. We're not humans here; we're broken specimens, and Lake Harmony is the repair shop. Everyone is subjected to the same repair process: Tear apart and rebuild.

"Proper nutrition may prevent macular degeneration and cataracts, the two leading causes of blindness in America . . ."

Sick of staring at the mess on my plate, I glance at the next table, where Sarah sits, watching me. In front of her is a plate with last night's spaghetti. Over the past few weeks we've gradually shifted seats to where we can look at each other. In this miserable world, seeing her face has slowly become one of the few small pleasures.

Sarah purses her lips sympathetically. Each night we "speak" to each other with facial expressions, slight movements of our foreheads, eyes, and lips.

"So how's dear old Dad?" Adam whispers, and leers at me from across the table. Joe is on the other side of the food hall, and Mr. Sparks is nowhere to be seen.

"Bet you enjoyed seeing the old man, huh?" Adam goes on. "The SOB who sent you here, right? You probably wanted to haul off and belt the guy."

It's a setup, plain and simple. On almost any other

day it would be easy to ignore. But not today, when I'm as raw and touchy as I've ever been. Part of me just wants to lash out at Adam and beat him into an unrecognizable pulp. And that part of me doesn't give a crap what the penalty for doing it would be.

"I heard Mom couldn't make it," Adam whispers. "Big disappointment, huh? Guess she was too busy shopping."

My pulse speeds up. I clench my fists under the table and take deep, slow breaths, trying to stay in control. I wish some chaperone were around to shut him up. Because if they don't, pretty soon I will.

"With crappy parents like that, you're probably better off here."

I launch up like a rocket, but as I do, the tops of my thighs unexpectedly hit the edge of the table and tilt it up. Plates of food slide and spill into the laps of the guys on Adam's side. Adam tries to get up, but the table has literally tilted against him. Out of the corner of my eye I see Joe and the troll already on the move, as if they knew this was coming.

Good. Let 'em come.

I reach across the table and grab Adam by the throat. His mouth opens and his eyes widen, and for an instant I see the real Adam, a scared bully who's all bluff when his henchmen aren't there to back him up. I've got the soft, unprotected flesh of his neck in my grip. Adam's hands go around my wrist as if to pry my fingers from his throat, but I tighten my grasp. His eyes start to bulge and his face turns red, and I can feel his carotid artery throbbing beneath my fingers. In that instant our eyes meet, and he knows I've seen the real Adam. A wimp in tough guy's clothing.

And just at that moment a single clear voice loudly but calmly warns: "It's a setup, you fool."

And yes, of course I knew that, and a moment ago I didn't care. But hearing Sarah say it changes something.

I let go of Adam's neck. He scrambles to his feet, raising his fists. "Come on, you big chicken! Let's see what you got."

It's almost comical. Adam waves his fists, his shirt stained red with splattered train crash. The other guys on his side of the table murmur angrily and wipe the spilled food off their laps. The guys on my side of the table grin. Joe and the troll stumble across the food hall like a couple of clowns. I step back from the table and watch. Suddenly, while there's chaos all around, I'm the calmest one in the bunch.

Adam drops his fists and goes stony, glaring daggers. "You're a dead man, Garrett."

Joe and the troll arrive. Sliding my hands into my pockets, I gaze over at Sarah and wink as both men, breathing hard, stop beside me. For a moment neither seems to know what to do.

"What . . . what's going on?" Joe stammers. "What happened here?"

Adam points at me. "He tried to pick a fight. He tried to choke me."

"Liar," I reply.

At the next table Sarah turns her head away, so as not to be caught smiling.

"Did anyone see what happened?" Joe asks.

By now the guys have straightened out the table. A few start to sit down again. Others complain about not getting enough to eat because their meals have spilled to the floor.

"Jon." Joe picks out a likely stooge. "You saw what happened, didn't you?"

"Uh . . ." Jon's eyes dart around. He knows he's supposed to help, but he isn't sure how. Not being included in the original plan means he's not certain who the target was. "Yeah, it was Pauly."

Joe grimaces. By now it's become a complete farce. He shoots me a look that says I may have gotten away with something this time, but it won't happen again.

The elation of escaping from Joe's latest trap is short-lived, and by the time we begin after-dinner Reflections, I've sunk into a deep funk. We open our notebooks and I begin to write about seeing my father and the disappointment I felt that my mom didn't come. But what I'm feeling is the sensation of free-falling into a dark, bottomless chasm of hopelessness. I'm stuck here.

After six months I'd be a fool to believe that Sabrina is sitting by the phone waiting for my call. All I can hope is that she still thinks about me. But how much longer will she even do that?

When no one is looking, I take out the brochure I grabbed in the administration building's lobby earlier in the day and secretly read it.

Other behavior-modification programs may

promise results, but Lake Harmony delivers. The child who returns from the Lake Harmony experience is the child you always knew you had.

It's a business, and as my mother would say, you can't stay in business if you don't produce a product. The product Lake Harmony delivers is the child you always knew you had, otherwise known as the one you wished you'd had, not the one you got stuck with. No one is going to spend four thousand dollars a month to get back the same kid they sent away. Garrett Durrell may walk out of here someday, but it won't be the Garrett Durrell I know. It'll be some zombie. Some mindless robot like Ron or Jon.

Kids come and go without explanation. One day Stu is gone and a fat, baby-faced guy named Miles replaces him. Miles has black tattooed bands around his biceps and newly shorn brown hair. You can imagine a much more menacing version of him with spiked hair, a smoldering cigarette, and a black jacket with chains. But without that costume he looks bewildered and frightened. In the dark after Shut Down he starts to sob.

"Shut up," Adam growls.

"I want to go home," Miles cries.

"And we want to sleep," Unibrow Robert snaps. "So shut it."

"You can't make me," Miles sobs.

And strangely he's right. At least for now. If anyone

gets out of bed, he'll set off a motion detector.

"You're dead," Adam warns.

The next morning when we run, Pauly is no longer the straggler. Now it's Miles, who complains that he has asthma and stops every fifty yards, red-faced and gasping, bent over with his hands on his knees. It's cold this morning. Not an early snap of fall frost, but an ominous icy presence under a sullen gray sky: the first real glimpse of the winter approaching. Our running path is blanketed by fallen yellow, red, and gold leaves, which crunch underfoot. The few leaves that remain hanging from the branches overhead are curled and brown. In the distance across a field some females are doing push-ups on their knees, their white breaths rising into a collective haze.

"Come on, you wimp!" Joe yells at Miles. "You want to go join the females?"

"No!" Miles gasps, and coughs. But his coughing sounds shallow and bogus.

"You're faking it, you fat little creep!" Joe yells.

"I'm not!" Miles whines.

Joe only runs sometimes, and when he does, like today, he hangs back, tormenting those who lag behind. But with Miles stopping every few moments, and Ron and Jon way out ahead, the line of runners stretches extra long and thin, and sometimes in the trees or behind a small rise there's no one else in sight.

"Garrett, wait up." Pauly catches up to me. "Frickin' freezing." His breaths are white mist.

"You don't say."

"New moon was . . . three nights ago." He gasps

out a few words with each breath as we jog between the dark trunks of trees. "It's getting colder . . . every day."

"Yeah."

"Next new moon . . . is in twenty-seven days. . . . Sarah and I are going . . . with or without you."

It's hard to imagine them getting very far. "You don't think it's already too cold?"

"Doesn't matter. . . . If Sarah doesn't go soon . . . she's never gonna go. . . . I'll kill myself before I . . . spend another . . . winter here."

For the first time, I believe him.

"You still think . . ." Pauly continues, "you can fool them?"

"No." We cross a low, muddy patch covered with a thin veneer of ice that crackles underfoot. The gummy mud beneath grabs at our heels.

"Then what . . . are you gonna do?" Pauly asks.

"Don't know."

"See . . . that's the thing. . . . You're still pretty strong. . . . You think you've got time . . . maybe something amazing will happen . . . your parents will change their minds . . . or Lake Harmony will get shut down . . . That's what . . . Sarah and I thought."

What if he's right?

"It won't happen . . . but by the time you figure that out . . . it'll be too late."

What if he's right?

"Believe me . . . Sarah and I know . . . because it's almost too late . . . for us."

"Suppose it works, Pauly. Suppose you get out of here. Where do you go?"

"Sarah has an aunt . . . in Toronto."

That's right. She mentioned an aunt when we were in the infirmary.

"If we can get to Canada . . . we'll be okay."

"You're going to walk to Canada?" I ask.

"We're somewhere . . . in upstate New York," Pauly gasps. "It can't . . . be that far. . . . Look, Sarah and I are going . . . whether you come . . . or not." He suddenly sounds impatient, even annoyed. But I sense that what spawns this is an inner strength, a steely determination you wouldn't expect from someone so meek and slight of stature. You have to admire someone who's willing to fight against these odds. After all, he's smart enough to know it's a crazy plan: Open the circuit-breaker box and shut off the power. Lock the box. Set a fire. Sneak out when the fire trucks come in. Somehow get to Canada with no money for food or transportation.

They don't stand a chance.

SEVENTEEN

"You will not touch anyone for any reason."

One evening in Reflections, Joe drops a piece of lined paper on the table in front of me. "Ready to try again?"

He means another letter to Sabrina.

"I . . ." I search for a way to stall. "I'm not sure."

The smile disappears from Joe's face. "Maybe another visit to TI would help."

Another trip to TI will simply postpone the inevitable. I'll come out and Joe will ask again if I'm ready to write the letter. If I don't, it'll be back to TI. The process repeated over and over until I'm a basket case.

I pick up a marker and begin to write:

Dear Sabrina,
This is the hardest letter I'll
ever write. I know you've been
wondering what happened to me. I
guess I could say I went away to
think.

Joe turns away to check on the other residents.

I . . .

I know what I'm expected to say. That I was wrong. I made a mistake. I'll never see her again. I don't love her.

I . . . Now that I've had time to
think, I realize that I was wrong
to

"Wrong to what, Garrett?" Coming from behind, the sudden sound of Joe's voice startles me. The marker falls out of my hand.

"Well?" he demands.

I can't . . .

"Pick up that marker and write!" he orders.

In the middle ages, one extreme form of capital punishment—usually reserved for criminals who'd committed treason or some other heinous offense—was being drawn and quartered. The victim was dragged, or "drawn," by four horses into a crowded public square. A rope or chain was tied from each wrist and ankle to a different horse. Then the horses were ordered to pull in opposite directions, the result being that the victim was literally torn into four separate parts.

I feel like my insides are being drawn and quartered. I know what I'm expected to do, but I can't. I know what will happen if I don't write this stupid letter, but I'm helpless to prevent it. The hope of seeing Sabrina is all I've got. If I give that up, I have nothing.

"Man, either you're a lot stupider than you look, or you're a glutton for punishment." Joe sounds almost as if he's in awe.

"I'm not, sir," I answer.

"Then prove it, smart guy."

The marker is motionless in my hand. No matter how I try, I can't make myself write.

"Prove it!" Joe shouts.

Back in TI. My chin has gone numb where it rests against the gritty floor. I guess I could move it, but then some other part of my face will just go numb. Same with all the parts of my body that are sore and hurting. What's the point of replacing one set of pains for another? *What did I do to deserve this?*

Endless hours pass with nothing but my thoughts to keep me company. No one comes in to grind my ankles and twist my legs. It's as if Joe doesn't want anything to distract me. The old tricks to pass the time don't work anymore. The CDs won't play in my head. The movies won't run. The same with childhood memories. I pull them into my consciousness, but they flicker and fade.

● ● ●

There was a woman named Sabrina once. She was new to the city and to her job. Being an introvert and a math geek—not the type to go to clubs or hang out in bars—she was lonely. A young man became her friend. He was thoughtful and attentive, and they had a lot in common . . .

Seems like a long time ago in a faraway place. Like a fairy tale. How long has it been? Seven months? Does she even think of me anymore?

Just write the damn letter and get it over with!

That voice in my head is not mine; it's Joe's. When did he become part of my consciousness?

What are you trying to prove? You know you can't win.

When I was a child, it was my parents' voices I heard in my head. Or the nanny's, since she was around more than they were. Or a teacher's. Now it's Joe's.

What's the point? She's probably forgotten you by now.

"Dear Sabrina. You haven't heard from me because I've gone away to think." Joe is reading from the letter I finally wrote to get out of TI. "Even though I really loved you once, I see now that I was wrong. I shouldn't have gotten involved with an older woman. I should have listened to my parents. When I come back, I won't be seeing you anymore. Sincerely, Garrett."

We're in Circle. When Joe finishes reading, he looks around and asks, "What do you think?"

Instead of the usual snide chorus of disapproval and

disbelief, there is silence. Pauly stares down at the floor, no doubt praying he won't be singled out. Sarah, bony and hollow-eyed, gazes at the blank wall as if she's not even there.

"Think I should send it?" Joe asks.

Chubby Rachel speaks up. "Why not?"

"Think he means it?" Joe asks.

No one answers.

"What do you think, Sarah?"

Sarah doesn't respond. Not even the slightest flicker in those empty eyes.

"Yo, stupid," Adam calls to her.

No reaction.

Joe holds up my letter to draw the attention back to him. "Anyone think Garrett really believes this?"

"Maybe it doesn't matter, as long as his girlfriend believes it," suggests Babyface Miles, the kid who cried at night for the first two weeks. Now there are no more tears. He's found a new family—not in Dignity with Joe as his "father," but in Adam's posse.

"You're saying it doesn't matter whether he means it?" Joe asks.

"It matters, but it's still gonna make it impossible for them to get back together," Miles says.

"That's not the point," Joe says. "Sabrina wasn't the problem. She was just a *symptom* of the problem. So you're only half right, Miles. Maybe we've taken away the symptom, but that doesn't mean we've solved the problem. What do you think would happen if Garrett got out of here now?" Joe may be asking Miles, but his eyes are firmly on me. "You think he's learned his lesson? You think he's truly owned up to all his mistakes? You think he's reached the point where he'll be respectful, polite, and obedient enough to return to his family?"

"I doubt it," says Adam.

"So do I," Joe says, turning now to face me. "I think it's a good step. It gets you back up to Level Two, Garrett. Keep up the good work. Maybe someday you'll get there."

"How's your B-ball, Garrett?" Mr. Sparks asks. It's pouring rain outside.

"Stone hands, sir," I answer.

He purses his lips. That wasn't what he wanted to hear. "But you play, right?"

"Not really, sir."

"A little?" he asks hopefully.

"Sorry, sir. Besides, I thought you had to be Level Four or higher to use the gym."

Mr. Sparks's eyes slide right and left to make sure no one's listening. "Listen, I got the saddest bunch of dweebs and no-talents you ever saw. We're one man short, and we need someone who'll make it a little challenging. A big guy to stand in the paint and put his hands up, got it?"

"That's about all I can do, sir."

"Way to go." Mr. Sparks actually claps his hand on my shoulder, and we walk toward the gym.

Turns out he wasn't kidding about the Level Fours and up being a feeble bunch of basketball players. But as with soccer, as soon as one kid drops out, Mr. Sparks becomes a player as well as the ref, and the rest of the game is basically just an excuse for him to run and gun and have some fun.

"Hey, thanks, Garrett," he says after the game. He's breathing hard, and his dark skin glistens with perspiration. His sweat-darkened T-shirt clings to his body, and he wears the satisfied smile of someone who's pushed himself to the edge of playful exhaustion. The other residents have gone, but Mr. Sparks has ordered me to stay behind and hold a rickety wooden ladder steady while he cranks up the backboards.

"For what, sir?" I ask.

"For being a good sport about it," he says. "I know it wasn't much fun for you."

"It beat studying, sir." I hold the ladder. Drops of his sweat make tiny splats on the gymnasium floor.

"Never got into the game, huh?" he says, with the touch of regret I have heard so many times in my life. As if it's some great tragedy that a guy with my size and build isn't some kind of athlete.

I give my standard reply: "Wasn't meant to be, sir."

"That's okay," Mr. Sparks says. "Important thing is to know yourself."

"Thought I did till I got here, sir."

Mr. Sparks's lips fold into a frown. He finishes cranking the backboard and climbs down the ladder, wiping sweat off his forehead with the back of his hand. "Listen, Garrett . . ." His voice drops. "I got a wife, a kid, and a sick mother to support. I need this gig, and it's not like there's a lot of steady work around here. There are things I'd say to you, but it could cost me my job. So I'll just say this: You gotta be true to yourself. I couldn't say that to most of the kids here, but I can to you. You gotta decide for yourself what's right and wrong. Don't let them decide for you."

"I'll be stuck here forever, sir," I remind him.

"Maybe not." Mr. Sparks closes the ladder. "You better get going."

I start across the gym toward the door, but when I'm halfway there, Mr. Sparks calls from behind: "One other thing, Garrett. Watch your back."

"Ahem." A throat clears. I'm in the bathroom before Shut Down. Adam is standing in the doorway. David Zitface, Unibrow Robert, and Babyface Miles are behind him. They're wearing the boots we're only supposed to wear for running. From his pocket Adam pulls out the pointed light-blue toothbrush shiv.

"What do you want?" I ask.

Adam gives me his best sinister smile. Those yellow reptilian teeth look ready to tear flesh. "I want you to beg for your life."

"Forget it. Go ahead and kill me. Put me out of my misery."

"My pleasure." Adam comes toward me.

"Just one thing," I add. "Let's see you do it without the backup squad."

"Doesn't work that way," Adam says.

"Oh, yeah? How's it work?"

"Like this."

He throws something. I was so busy watching the shiv in his left hand that I didn't notice what he was doing with his right. Something soft hits my face and bursts into a light orange cloud. Instantly I'm blinded; my eyes, nose, and throat are on fire. It tastes like hot peppers. *Wham!* In the blind darkness I'm slammed against the wall and pummeled by a barrage of fists and kicking boots. Unable to see, with jagged jabs of pain coming from all sides, I sink to the floor and curl into a ball, trying to protect my head with my arms. The fists and kicks continue. All hurt. Some worse than others. A punch produces a dull throbbing pain in my shoulder. A vicious kick results in a sudden screaming jolt at my hip that makes me grimace and cower. I keep my back to the wall and my head covered, taking most of the blows on my shins and forearms. My eyes tear, but more from the burning powder than the pain.

The beating continues. When I cover my face with my arms and protect my stomach by tucking in my legs, they stomp on my head and ribs. I can taste blood on my lips, though I'm not sure where it's coming from. They're crazy to do this. I'll be covered with telltale bruises. But maybe they don't care.

A boot connects with my head. The pain explodes and blurs.

I'm gone for a moment, then back, then gone again. Am I blacking out?

Out of nowhere a voice says, "That's enough." The blows stop, but it's too late. I'm fading into darkness. Strange though, that the voice . . . sounded like Joe's.

EIGHTEEN

"Success at Lake Harmony can only be achieved by changing your attitude."

I wake up in the dark, uncertain where I am, flooded with aches and pains. There are deep crevices of hot agony where my body feels as if it's working overtime to start the healing process. There's an odd smell in the air, and it takes a moment to place it: stale cigarette smoke. Guess it makes sense that I'd be in the infirmary. Then the darkness grows blurry and I'm gone again.

"Garrett?" A whispered voice wakes me. I open my eyes and find Mr. Sparks beside the cot. He's wearing a heavy blue baseball jacket zipped to the neck as if he's just come in from outside. The infirmary is the dull gray of predawn.

"How are you?" His face is stony. No sign of the usual smile.

My lips are cracked and my throat feels dry. Guess I've been breathing through my mouth because my nose is swollen. Moving my jaw to speak hurts. "Never been better, sir."

"Man." Mr. Sparks shakes his head. "I've never seen anyone get it as bad as you."

"Did Joe order it, sir?" I ask.

Mr. Sparks hesitates. "No."

"But he stopped it, sir."

"Yeah."

"Adam and his gang in trouble, sir?" I ask.

Mr. Sparks shakes his head.

"I don't get it, sir."

"It's all about results, Garrett. You think this place could stay in business with parents shelling out four grand a month if they didn't see results?"

"What about Sarah, sir?"

"An exception to the rule. Most parents give this place a year or a year and a half at best. No results, they pull the kid and try something else."

"What's that got to do with Adam, sir?" I ask.

"Mr. Z and Joe, the other group leaders . . . their hands are tied. There's only so much they're allowed to do. State and federal regulations, you know? So they use Adam and his boys to do the rest. If Adam's got a grudge against you and decides to do some freelancing, what can Joe do? They both know that without thugs like Adam there's no more Lake Harmony."

"Sir, did a kid really die here a couple of years ago?" I ask.

Mr. Sparks nods slowly.

"How, sir?"

"Official cause of death was listed as heatstroke. State did an investigation and Lake Harmony was cleared of responsibility. I hear the parents have brought a civil suit, but those things take years, and there's insurance to cover it."

"Was it really heatstroke, sir?"

"Sure. You force an overweight kid to run in the sun for six hours on a hundred-degree day and heatstroke is pretty much guaranteed. The group leader got fired, the state completed its investigation, and life went back to normal."

The infirmary slowly brightens as the day begins. Outside, car tires crunch over gravel. Mr. Sparks raises his head alertly. "Gotta go."

"Wait, sir. Why'd you come see me?" I ask.

Mr. Sparks looks down at me with as grave an expression as I've ever seen on his face. "From now on you gotta be careful, Garrett. I mean it. Real careful."

They keep me in the infirmary for four days. Just before lunch on the fourth day, Ron arrives to take me back. In the food hall, I get stared at hard. And no wonder. My face is swollen, bruised, and black and blue.

At the Dignity table, Adam and David Zitface sit opposite me. Babyface Miles is on my right and

Unibrow Robert on my left. No words are spoken. It's all facial expressions. Sneers and smirks. Mr. Sparks hovers nearby, trying to stay within range while not appearing obvious about it.

"Ahem." Adam clears his throat, then places his hands on the table and slowly balls them into fists. Miles, David, and Robert do the same. Their knuckles are swollen and scabbed.

From beating on me.

Their smiles say they'll be glad to do it again.

That evening after Reflections we line up to go back to the dorm. Toward the end of the line, Pauly squeezes in front of me and behind Miles and Adam. He's made no attempt to communicate all day, but now he gives me a hurried wink. As usual, Joe is at the rear, where he can watch us.

As we enter the hall outside the dorm, Pauly suddenly stumbles forward into Miles, knocking him into Adam. All three fall down and become a tangle of arms and legs.

"Hey!" Joe pushes past me and bends over to pull the boys apart. Pauly is the first to crawl out of the pile. He pops to his feet and races toward me, eyes wide. Then he's behind me, pushing me toward Joe, Adam, and the others just hard enough to give me the idea of what he wants me to do. It all happens so fast, I hardly have time to think. I pretend to stumble forward and "trip" into Adam, knocking him on his butt and landing hard on top of him. With considerable pleasure I hear him gasp and then moan in pain.

"Get up!" Joe shoves Miles aside and steps over Adam and me. He starts pulling at our arms and legs, but I pretend to lose my balance and fall on Adam again.

"Get off!" Adam squirms under me. I jam my elbow into his neck and my knee into his ribs while I pretend to get my footing. Everyone in the family has turned to watch. They must assume this is my revenge for the beating. Is that why Pauly decided tonight was the night? Because everyone would be expecting this?

In the midst of trying to separate Adam and me, Joe suddenly stops and stares down the hall. Pauly has pulled open the breaker panel. Joe lets go of Adam and me and lunges toward him.

Up to this moment I haven't actually committed to Pauly's plan. The worst I could be accused of is getting a few revenge licks on Adam. But if I don't do something to stop Joe right now, he's going to get to Pauly before there's time to shut off the power and lock the box.

NINETEEN

"You will endeavor to rise through the levels necessary for graduation."

I reach out, grab Joe's ankle, and yank him back.

The hall goes pitch-black, and there's a metallic bang as Pauly slams the breaker box shut. Then a softer click as he closes the small padlock. Meanwhile guys start bumping into each other, sputtering and swearing in the confusion.

I feel a hand pulling on my arm and hard breaths against my ear as Pauly whispers, "Go to the food hall! Get as much as you can! Meet me behind the bushes near the flagpole."

Then he vanishes into the dark.

The hall has grown quieter. It feels like fewer people are around. I hear footsteps, whispers. A door slams. Someone laughs.

"Get a flashlight!" Joe's voice pierces the dark.

Bang! Bang! Loud, metallic banging rings through the air. Could be Joe slamming on the circuit-breaker box. Or maybe it's something else.

Crash! Somewhere down the hall glass breaks.

"Yee-ha!" someone cries with glee.

"The infirmary!" someone else yells.

Running footsteps. More crashes. Joe curses under his breath.

Doors open and slam. Without electricity, the forty-five-second automatic lockdown doesn't work. Nor do the motion detectors and alarms. In the dark I grope my way down the hall until my hands feel the panic bar on a door. I push hard and the door flies open. Outside the fall air is chilly. The sky overhead glitters with more sparkling stars than I've ever seen. For a moment, despite the insanity around me, the sight of all those stars is fantastic.

A loud crash followed by shrieks of laughter pulls me back to reality. I press myself into the darkness against a wall and listen. There are voices in the night, and yelling; the sounds of running and heavy breathing. Staying close to the wall, I work my way toward the food hall.

I'm stuffing stale rolls into a plastic bag when the lights burst on and alarms start to ring loudly. Time to get moving. Squinting in the brightness, I push through a door. Outside it's not nearly as dark as before. The outdoor lights are on, creating bright spots everywhere. I try to stay in the dark. A pair of kids races past. The whoop of a car alarm catches me by surprise. Unbelievable! Someone is trying to break into a car. Shouts, cries, crazed laughter, and breaking glass fill the air. Some of these kids aren't even trying to escape; they're just going on a rampage.

The heavy scent of smoke catches me by surprise. Next comes the distant wail of sirens. Amazing! Pauly really did it. Staying in the shadows behind the buildings, I make my way toward the front gate. Ahead is the basketball court, then the flagpole rising into the darkness. Two shapes are huddled behind the bushes next to the pole.

Bodies flit through the light and shadows—kids running this way and that, enjoying a brief taste of anarchy. A loud metallic clang rings out from a building close by. No idea what it could be.

I duck down and scamper from the corner of the building to the bushes. Pauly sees me coming.

"Hey," he whispers as I squat down with him and Sarah. "Glad you could make it."

Sarah smiles. Even in the dark her eyes are bright with determination and hope, but her smile is tight and frightened. In the distance the sirens gradually grow louder.

"You got some food?" Pauly whispers.

I shake the bag. "Stale rolls."

"Okay." Pauly has a plastic bag too.

"Now what?" I ask.

He jerks his head. Fifty yards away, half a dozen chaperones, "fathers," and "mothers" have gathered at the tall metal gate. The sirens are growing louder, and now we can see flashing red lights in the dark distance. The smell of smoke surrounds us.

"Why don't they open the gate?" Sarah whispers.

"Because they know kids are gonna make a run for it," Pauly answers.

The sirens grow louder and the flashing lights brighter, illuminating the bare branches of trees. As soon as the first set of headlights appears down the road, the chaperones unlock the gate and push it open. A split second later a kid bursts out of the dark, running as fast as he can for freedom. A chaperone tackles him, and another helps subdue him by grabbing his arm and twisting it sharply. Next come two girls. Both are caught by male chaperones and handed over, clawing and screaming, to female group leaders.

It's like a serious version of capture the flag. Each time a kid is caught trying to escape, it takes a chaperone or group leader to drag him or her away. The number of chaperones and leaders left dwindles. With flashing lights and bellowing exhaust, the first fire engine rumbles through the gate. Pauly rises into a squat.

"They have to clear a path for the fire trucks," he whispers. "As soon as the next one comes through, we run for it."

The next truck is a long hook and ladder.

"Now!" Pauly hisses. As the hook and ladder rolls through, we sprint in the dark toward the gate. The remaining chaperones and group leaders can't see us because the long truck blocks their view. I make it through the gate and keep running toward the shadowy woods. A second later I crash into the brush and through the branches, slowing so that I don't accidentally smash into a tree in the dark.

I can hear feet behind me kicking through the dry, crackling leaves. It should be Pauly and Sarah, but I'm afraid to stop and look in case it's not.

"Pauly!" Sarah cries somewhere in the dark behind us. Spinning around, I see Pauly running about twenty feet behind me. Beyond him Sarah's silhouette is coming toward us through the trees, backlit by the red and white swirling lights of the fire trucks. But she's not alone. Someone is behind her and catching up fast. It's difficult to tell in the dark, but I have a feeling it's Joe. Pauly gives me an alarmed look. If we run, Sarah will get caught. We'll get away because Joe can't possibly get us while he's holding onto her.

"Ahhh!" Less than a dozen yards away, Sarah cries out as Joe tackles her. They crash down into leaves and twigs. With Sarah on the ground, Joe quickly jumps back to his feet. But before he can yank her up, he's got company—me.

I grab his wrist and twist his arm behind him in the classic Lake Harmony restraint. To my surprise he doesn't resist.

Sarah gets up and hurries away until she's well out of reach. Pauly comes back through the dark. For a moment we stand among the tree trunks and brush. Yells and shouts filter toward us through the woods from the grounds of Lake Harmony.

"You can't get away," Joe snarls. I feel his chest enlarge as he takes a deep breath. Before he can yell, I clamp my hand over his mouth, muffling him. Now he starts to struggle. I twist his arm more tightly behind his back and push him down to the leaf-covered ground, pressing one knee against his back. He squirms, and I tighten my hold.

"Stop or I'll break your arm," I warn him.

A muffled croak squeezes out from between my fingers. Sounds like, "Go ahead."

I tighten my hand over his mouth and use my weight to press him facedown into the leaves. A woodsy scent rises into my nostrils as I feel so much repressed anger bubble up from inside. In my grip is the person who has caused me so many months of pain and agony. So many months of despair. The person who allowed me to be beaten within an inch of my life. I bend over and whisper into his ear. "You of all people ought to be more respectful, Joe. Didn't anyone ever teach you to be polite and obedient? Keep behaving like this and you'll wind up in TI."

He squirms, and I press my knee down harder, leaning all my weight into his back. All those months wasted . . . agonized over . . . how I hated it. This anger has been building up without my realizing it. Maybe I was wrong not to let it out like the others. Hell, I wound up spending just as much time in TI as they did anyway. Mostly because of this SOB. I push Joe down even harder. He squirms. *How does it feel, you lousy miserable sadistic bastard?*

Joe jerks and makes another croaking sound. I feel fingers on my shoulder and look up in the dark. It's Sarah, her face ghostly. "Easy," she cautions. "You don't want to kill him."

"Yeah, I do. After what he did to me."

Joe tries to say something. I yank him up, then slam him down against the ground. "And don't give me that 'I was just doing my job' crap either," I tell him.

"Hey, come on," Pauly says in a rushed voice, joining Sarah. "This isn't about revenge. It's about escape."

He reaches into his plastic bag and pulls out half a roll of duct tape. Ripping a piece off, he presses it over Joe's mouth. We use more of it to bind his hands behind his back, and the rest goes around his ankles. Then we drag him deeper into the woods and behind a large fallen tree trunk—a place where we hope he won't be found until morning.

Pausing to catch my breath, I notice for the first time the short plumes of white vapor that escape our lips. It's cold, and the woods are quiet and dark. Way darker than any city or suburb can ever be. The only sounds coming from the direction of Lake Harmony are the loud grumble of a fire engine and the squeal of air brakes. It sounds like the uprising has been quelled.

"This way." Pauly points in the dark.

"How do you know?" I ask. Other than a general feeling for the way back to Lake Harmony, I have no sense of direction.

Pauly points up through the bare branches at the dark glittering sky. "North Star."

• • •

Eight hours later the sky is dressed in predawn gray and the woods are filled with mist. Hidden by the trees about thirty feet from the edge of a two-lane road, the three of us hug our knees to our chests, our teeth chattering softly. Our shirts and pants are damp with dew. Our feet, in Lake Harmony flip-flops, are scratched and dirty from trudging all night through the woods.

"Can't we sleep?" Sarah asks with a shivering yawn, her lips blue from the cold.

"We have to keep going," Pauly replies with a determination that belies his frail appearance.

"How far do you think we've gone?" Sarah asks.

Pauly gives me a quizzical look. "What do you think?"

"Not that far," I answer. "Maybe four or five miles. It was pretty slow in the woods."

A distant rumble breaks the silence. Sounds like a truck. "Wait here." Pauly creeps through the brush to the edge of the woods. The roar increases until a big eighteen-wheeler thunders past, rattling the dry branches of the trees and shaking loose a few dead brown leaves. Pauly comes back. "It had Ontario plates. I think we're on the road to Canada. Won't take long if we hitchhike."

"You sure you want to do that?" I ask. "The news must be out. Anybody sees three kids hitchhiking in these clothes, won't they know exactly where we're from?"

"Not yet," Pauly says. "Maybe never. If there's any news, it won't be out until later this morning. But I bet that's not gonna happen. Think about it, Garrett. Lake

Harmony can't afford to let parents know that kids can escape. They'll do everything they can to keep it out of the media."

"How can they stop it?" Sarah asks.

The irony of the answer makes me grin. "Crisis management. It's what my mom does for a living. She keeps bad news out of the media."

"Right," Pauly agrees. "They'll tell the employees not to talk. There will only be a rumor that there was some kind of disturbance last night. But we still have to book as fast as we can."

"I still don't see how we can hitchhike," I tell him. "Who's gonna pick up two guys and a girl?"

Pauly smiles impishly. "You'll see." He tells Sarah to stand by the side of the road with her thumb out while he and I crouch in a ditch nearby. And wouldn't you know, the first vehicle to come along is a bright red pickup with an expanded cab. The driver is about Joe's age, with a red plaid shirt and a long brown ponytail, his broad belly pushed up against the bottom of the steering wheel. At first he looks more than a little annoyed when Pauly and I pop up out of the ditch. But then he shrugs and mutters, "Should've known."

"Where you headed?" Pauly asks, holding the passenger door open.

"Alexandria Bay," the driver answers.

"That north?" Pauly asks.

The driver studies him for a moment. "Not from around here, huh?"

"Is it toward Canada?"

"Yeah, it's toward Canada," the driver says.

"Great."

Sarah and Pauly climb in the back and leave the front passenger seat for me. The driver rolls his eyes slightly, as if to say the least we could do was let Sarah keep him company in the front. The pickup pulls back onto the road. To our right the predawn sky slowly brightens as the sun prepares to make its daily appearance. Pauly has already warned us to let him do most of the talking. Suddenly I become aware of chattering teeth behind me. Must be Pauly and Sarah. The driver hears it too and turns up the heat.

"So, where you kids from?" he asks in what I assume is the standard "I'll give you a ride if you'll give me conversation" opening.

"Miami," Pauly says.

"Salt Lake," answers Sarah.

"New York," I add. "City."

"No kidding? What are you all doing up here?"

"Uh, following a band," Pauly says, giving his prefab answer to the question he knew we'd be asked.

"Which one?" the driver asks.

"A jam band you probably haven't heard of," Pauly said. "Called Fudge."

"You kidding me?" the guy says, clearly pleased. "I know Fudge. After Jerry died and Phish broke up, who the hell else you gonna listen to? I'll say this, friend, you got good taste in music." He goes quiet for a moment, then adds in a puzzled way, "Only I'm pretty sure they're doing a West Coast tour right now."

Silence. Things looked good until Pauly got caught

in that lie. Now what? The driver glances at me with a slightly hurt expression on his face, as if it's not fair that he'd give us a ride and we'd lie to him.

"So, uh, guess that's not why you're headed to Canada," he says, looking again in the rearview mirror. Only now I'm pretty sure he's noticing that Pauly and I are wearing identical clothes, and that I have bruises and black and blue marks on my face. Next he glances down at my feet, no doubt inspecting the flip-flops.

"I know a guy who works over at that school in Lake Harmony," he says. "The one with the double fence running around it. Know the one I'm talking about?"

TWENTY

"The smallest gesture of disrespect will result in demerits."

No one answers.

"They send spoiled rich kids there," the driver continues. "Most of 'em have drug problems or are just plain troublemakers. There were plenty of kids like that when I was growing up. Only nobody had the money to send them to fancy schools. Usually they just got kicked out of the house. Parents said they'd be welcome home once they learned how to behave. Most got back in line pretty quick, but a few left town and we never saw them again."

We ride along without talking. When the scattered

clouds to the right begin to turn pink, I know that we are indeed headed north. After that cold night in the woods, the warmth of the pickup's cab is soothing, and I'm glad we're covering so many miles this way rather than on sore feet in flip-flops. But now a new sensation begins to take hold: hunger. There are rolls in my bag, but after that sleepless night, I'd do anything for some coffee. For the first time in almost seven months, that's not just a fruitless dream. It might actually be possible.

A sparkling gold sun rises in the east. The scattered clouds go from pink to white as the sky turns a lighter shade of blue. In the warm cab, with the steady rumble of the engine, my eyelids feel heavy, and I slouch down and let the back of my head rest against the seat.

A little while later the pickup starts to slow. Opening my eyes, I see a gas station with a convenience store ahead on the right. The driver pulls up to the pump. Without a word he gets out. Sarah, Pauly, and I swivel our heads to watch as he starts to fill the tank. Leaving the hose running, he comes over to the window. "I'm gonna get some coffee. Want anything?"

The three of us exchange looks.

"I'd love some coffee," Sarah says. "With milk and sugar."

"Me too," I agree. It's a dream come true.

"No, thanks," Pauly says, tersely.

"How about something to eat?" the driver asks. "Doughnuts?"

"Sure, great, thanks."

"Be right back." He heads into the shop.

As soon as the driver is out of sight, Pauly reaches for the door. "We gotta run."

"What?" This catches me completely by surprise.

"He's calling the cops," Pauly says.

"What are you talking about?" I ask.

"Come on," Pauly says impatiently. "You heard him. He's got a friend who works at Lake Harmony. What the hell do you think he's doing?"

"Getting us coffee and doughnuts," Sarah says.

"No way." Pauly shakes his head adamantly.

"Why not?" I ask.

"'Cause he doesn't give a crap about us," Pauly says. "It's his friend he's thinking about. I don't know about you, but I'm out of here."

He pushes open the door and starts to get out. Sarah and I share a look.

"What do you think?" I ask.

Sarah shrugs.

"I think he's wrong," I tell her. "But if *I'm* wrong, we're busted."

Sarah glances at the storefront. The door is closed and we can't see inside. The driver could be getting us coffee. Or he could be on the phone.

Pauly is out of the truck now. He sticks his face in the window. "You really want to risk it? What do you think is gonna happen if we get caught and sent back?"

It kills me to give up that coffee, but Sarah and I get out. There's a cornfield across the road. The stalks are wilted and brown, but they're tall and thick and a good place to hide. We scamper into the field, our flip-flops catching in the soft, moist dirt. Finally we stop and peek back through the stalks. Goose bumps race up and down our arms as the cold air once again envelops us.

Across the road the driver comes out of the shop carrying a gray cardboard tray with coffees and a bag of doughnuts. Halfway to the pickup he stops and frowns, then starts to look around.

"It could still be a trap," Pauly whispers, although without as much conviction as before.

The driver slowly shakes his head, then puts the coffee and doughnuts on the front seat of the pickup and finishes pumping the gas. He gets back in the truck and drives off.

A bird chirps somewhere in the cornfield. In the distance a rooster crows. Sarah's teeth have begun to chatter again. "Now what?" she asks.

Back on the road a long semi barrels past.

"We'll just do trucks," Pauly says. "Semis. That way there's a good chance the drivers won't be from around here. They're only passing through."

Pauly may have some weird ideas, but he has some good ones too. We creep back to the edge of the cornfield. When another semi appears in the distance, Sarah gets out on the road and does her thing. Once again the driver isn't happy when Pauly and I appear, but he agrees to take us just the same. The good news is he speaks French and hardly any English.

We ride for a while. By now it's past breakfast and we're hungry, so we break out the stale rolls. It's not easy to eat them with nothing to drink, but we do our best. The truck driver watches impassively, saying nothing. And now there's another problem.

"I have to use the bathroom," Sarah whispers. Pauly nods in agreement.

A little while later a truck stop appears in the distance.

"Could we stop for the bathroom?" Pauly asks the driver, who frowns.

"*La toilette*," Sarah says in French.

The driver nods and pulls off at the truck stop, but not, I notice, at the gas pumps. We get out, but as we walk across the parking lot toward the restaurant, we hear the throaty rev of the semi's diesel engine. The truck starts out of the parking lot without us. Can't say I'm surprised.

As we cross the asphalt in our flip-flops, I notice that our feet are filthy brown—a telltale sign that we're on the run. Inside the restaurant the scent of bacon and coffee is almost dizzying. I gaze enviously at the people in booths eating. For a moment I just stand there. After all that time in Lake Harmony my brain has been rewired enough that I automatically wait to be told what to do.

"We'll use the bathrooms, then figure out what to do next," Pauly suggests.

In the bathroom Pauly and I each go into a stall. A few moments later, when I open the stall door to leave, I catch a glimpse of a man in a cowboy hat who's pressed close to a urinal. As he turns his head in my direction, I quickly pull the stall door closed.

The toilet flushes in the stall next to me. "Pauly,"

I whisper, hoping my voice is covered by the swirling water.

"What?"

"Don't leave the stall."

He's smart enough not to ask why. I count slowly to fifty and then push the door open a crack. The cowboy-hat guy is gone.

"All clear," I whisper.

Pauly comes out and asks in a low voice. "Who?"

"Someone at the urinal reminded me of the guy who brought me to Lake Harmony."

We stop at the sinks to wash our hands and faces.

"Think he could be looking for us?" Pauly asks, drying his face with paper towels.

"If they hire him to bring kids to Lake Harmony, there's no reason they wouldn't use him to bring kids back."

At the bathroom door I stop and peek out. There's no sign in the lobby of anyone wearing a cowboy hat. Pauly and I find Sarah near a news rack scanning a local paper.

"Anything about Lake Harmony?" Pauly asks in a low voice.

She shakes her head.

Just then Rebecca strolls around the corner, gazing down at a magazine.

TWENTY-ONE

"Any violation of the rules will result in demerits."

My heart stops. She's barely a dozen feet away. I turn and pretend to look at the paperbacks in the rack. Pauly and Sarah have sense enough to realize something is wrong, and they also quickly turn away. When I raise my head again, Rebecca is gone.

"Who was that?" Sarah whispers.

"One of the transporters my parents hired to bring me to Lake Harmony," I answer.

"Split up and walk out one at a time," Pauly whispers. "We'll meet behind the Dumpsters in the back."

"Try to walk out close to other people," I suggest, "so it looks like you're with them."

We head in different directions and one by one leave the truck stop. Outside, the sun has risen higher, and the air isn't quite as chilly. We meet by the Dumpsters, which stink of old garbage and are so full that bags and boxes poke out from under the lids.

"See anyone?" Sarah asks, arms crossed, hugging herself.

"No, but they've got to be looking for us," I answer.

"How far do you think we are from Canada?" she asks.

Pauly shrugs and stares down at the brown banana peels and squashed lemon rinds on the ground. "Can't be far. Half the cars parked in front have Canadian license plates."

"We're gonna have to stay off the roads," I tell them.

"And go at night," adds Pauly.

"I can't spend another night in the woods," Sarah says. "I'll freeze. And what about food?"

The answers to these questions are not readily forthcoming. Canada may not be that far away, but without money and food and warm clothes, it might as well be across an ocean.

Pauly sniffs and glances at the Dumpster. A crooked smile crosses his lips. "I think we just found dinner."

In the trees behind the truck stop we push together dry leaves to rest on until dark. In our short-sleeved shirts the leaves and twigs are itchy and uncomfortable. Still, it isn't long before Pauly's breathing becomes steady in a way that suggests he's asleep. I lie quietly and watch a small ant crawl up a thin brown twig.

Sarah wiggles, trying to get comfortable. We're facing each other. Despite the thinness of her face, the dark rings around her eyes, and the raggedness of her short black hair, she's still a pretty girl.

"Can't sleep?" I whisper.

"Never was the outdoors type," she whispers back.

"What do you think Pauly will do when he gets to Canada?" I ask.

"Huh?" Her pale forehead wrinkles.

"Think your aunt will let him stay with her too?"

"Oh . . . uh, for a little while, I hope. Then he'll have to decide. Anything's better than Lake Harmony, right?"

"Definitely," I agree.

"What about you?" Sarah asks.

"Go back to New York, I guess. But not to my parents. At least not unless they promise not to send me away again."

"I bet you can't wait to see Sabrina," she says.

With a start I realize it's been days since I last thought of her.

"How did you meet?" Sarah asks.

"At the beginning of last year . . . no, wait, I mean, two years ago. I keep forgetting where I've spent the last seven months."

Sarah nods. "Who wants to remember?"

I gaze at her eyes, more bright and lively than they ever were at Lake Harmony. "What about you? Almost three years."

"We're not talking about me," Sarah answers.

"We're talking about you and Sabrina."

"She was a new teacher at my school. It was this instantaneous thing for me. I'd sit in class in a daze. A schoolboy crush, you know?"

Sarah smiles. "But it turned out to be more."

I nod. The leaves under my ear are scratchy.

"How did it happen?"

"I kept making excuses to stay after class. I was sure that sooner or later she'd figure out what was going on and blow me off. But it didn't happen. I started to get the feeling she was looking forward to seeing me. She was new to the city, and I guess it was kind of lonely. But it was still weird. Like I couldn't believe she'd even be interested in being friends. And I guess she was having a hard time believing it, too."

"I bet." Sarah grins.

"So it turned out we're both major fans of manga and graphic novels, you know? And she mentioned that she'd discovered this great bookstore downtown—"

"So you went, hoping to run into her?"

I nod and feel my face grow warm.

"That's so cute!" she whispers.

How strange is it that even lying here shivering on the cold ground and scratchy leaves, my body sore and hungry, the memory of that time momentarily warms and fills me?

"So one day she showed up at the store, right?" Sarah guesses.

I nod. "It didn't take long. Later she told me she had a feeling she might find me there."

"And?" Sarah asks, eagerly.

"She said we could be friends. And we were for maybe a couple of months, but then it changed. We started meeting after school. Nothing else mattered. I just wanted to be with her every possible second."

The smile fades from Sarah's face. "She was your teacher. You didn't try to hide it?"

"We did, but not very well," I admit. "I mean, try to understand. We were swept up in it. It wasn't like we sat around trying to think logically."

"So what happened?"

"People saw us together. The rumors started. My parents found out. They went to the headmaster and got her fired."

"Oh, God."

"I was so pissed at them. I guess they thought getting Sabrina fired would be the end of it, but that just made me want to see her more. And by then it was out in the open, so I started staying over at her apartment."

"Isn't it against the law?" Sarah asks. "I mean, you're a minor."

"Be honest. Do I look, or act, like a 'minor' to you?"

Sarah shakes her head.

"Seriously. It wasn't like one of us was taking advantage of the other. We just really liked each other and had a lot in common."

"But couldn't your parents have gone to the police?" Sarah asks.

"They threatened to, but they never did."

"Why not?"

"They were afraid more people would find out. They both have big jobs. My mom especially. Her whole business is about helping people avoid bad publicity. So she's totally insane when it comes to anything negative about herself. I think she was worried that if the case went to court it would look really bad. Like if she's so good at what she does, how come she couldn't keep her own son out of the news?"

"So when you started staying at Sabrina's . . . that's when your parents began thinking about Lake Harmony?" Sarah guesses.

"Right. They got completely unhinged. Like if they didn't get me away from her instantly, it would ruin my life."

"Or your mom's," Sarah adds archly.

"Exactly." I yawn, and feel my eyes start to close.

Someone is shaking my shoulder. "Rise and shine."

I open my eyes. It's dark and cold. I close my eyes and curl up more tightly. The last thing I want to do is get up.

The hand shakes my shoulder again. "Come on, Garrett."

Leaves crackle beneath my elbows as I slowly prop myself up. Crickets chirp, and somewhere in the distance an owl is hooting. I'm hungry. For the past twenty-four hours all I've eaten is some bread.

Pauly is a dark shadow. Sarah is beside him, hugging herself to stay warm, her teeth chattering again.

"Ah-choo!" Pauly sneezes and sniffs.

"Bless you," I respond automatically as I slowly get to my feet.

Sarah chuckles. "I remember the first time I heard you say that. The food hall, remember?"

"Like I could forget?" I answer.

"I said to myself, 'Anyone who says "bless you" doesn't belong at Lake Harmony.'"

"Too bad no one else felt that way," I say.

"Time to Dumpster dive." Pauly leads us back to the truck stop. The smell of garbage grows stronger as we get closer to the big dark-green containers. White and black garbage bags overflow from under the lids.

"Ah-choo!" Pauly sneezes again and wipes his nose on his arm. He glances at the Dumpster. "Anyone ever done this?"

"It was your idea," Sarah reminds him.

Pauly lets out a sigh. "Okay. Garrett, you hold it."

I push the heavy metal lid up, and Pauly reaches in and pulls out a large black bag. He tears it open, and out spill broken egg shells, coffee grounds, soggy crusts of sandwiches, and other half-eaten food. But while the Dumpster may smell like rotten garbage, the thrown-out food in the bags appears fairly fresh. It still looks incredibly gross, but the nearness to nourishment—any kind of nourishment—causes my stomach to growl. One triangle of leftover club sandwich looks relatively untouched. I pick it up and take a bite. Pauly and Sarah both make faces.

"How's it taste?" Sarah asks.

"Not bad."

Pauly finds some French fries, and Sarah tentatively tries half a bagel and cream cheese. At the taste of food our appetites grow stronger and our inhibitions weaker. By the end we've feasted as well, if not better, than we ever did at Lake Harmony.

Pauly even burps. I can't help smiling.

"What's so funny?" Sarah asks.

"Pauly Dumpster diving," I answer. "I don't think anyone at Lake Harmony would believe it."

"I'm not sure I would believe it," Pauly says with a grin.

The big black garbage bags contain food, but the medium-size white ones hold mostly packaging and receipts from the gift shop. You can empty a white one, turn it inside out, punch holes for your head and arms, and the result is a thin plastic vest. Before long each of us is wearing a four-ply bag vest made of two white ones on the inside and two black ones on the outside.

"I can't wait to take a shower," Sarah mumbles as we begin to trek north just inside the woods that line the side of the road. It's difficult to walk in the dark. We trip over unseen branches, get pricked and scratched by vines and brambles, and stub our unprotected toes on rocks. Now and then the distant headlights of a car send spooky, moving shadows through the tree trunks, and we duck down and wait until the lights pass.

"Can't we walk along the road?" Sarah complains after stubbing her toe on a tree stump.

"Too much chance of being seen," Pauly says. "They know we'll be traveling at night."

"Maybe later," I suggest, "when there are fewer cars."

We continue to struggle through the dark woods.

"Ow!" Suddenly Sarah lets out a cry and crashes down into the underbrush and dry leaves. She curls on her side, clutching her foot with both hands and whimpering. Pauly and I kneel beside her. "What's wrong?"

"I stepped on something," she sobs, clearly in great pain. "It's stuck in my foot. Get it out!"

"Still have those matches?" I ask Pauly.

"Yeah." There's a scratching sound, then a small burst of yellow flame. I slip the flip-flop off Sarah's dirty foot. Her sole is a dark, reddish mud of dirt and blood.

"Ow! Ow! *Ow!*" She wails in agony.

"Hold still," I tell her. "It's hard to see."

"Crap!" Pauly lets go of the match, which must have burned down to his fingertips.

"I need light," I tell him.

He lights another match, but in its dim flicker it's hard to find where the bleeding is coming from, and before I can locate the problem, that match burns out too.

"It hurts!" Sarah cries. "Please get it out!"

"We're gonna run out of matches," Pauly says.

"Make a small fire with leaves," I tell him.

"They'll see it."

"Come on, she's hurt."

Pauly bunches some leaves together and strikes a match. They ignite, and the air fills with the smell of smoke. I spit into my hands and wipe the dirt and blood from Sarah's trembling foot. A pointed piece of wood the width of a thin pencil is stuck in her heel. It went right through her flip-flop before it broke off.

"Oh, God!" Sarah cries when I pull it out. "Oh, Lord!"
A second later she moans with relief and massages her
foot. In the flickering light of the fire her face is streaked
with tears and smudged with blood and dirt. Bits of
crumpled leaves stick to her cheek. I brush them away.
Sarah looks at me with reddened, watery eyes.

"How's it feel?" I ask.

"Better, thanks."

"Garrett!" Pauly grabs my arm.

The fire has begun to spread beyond the little pile
of leaves Pauly made. It crackles and flares as it creeps
outward in a circle. Pauly starts to stamp out the flames
with his flip-flops. I join him, and the air fills with smoke
and the chemical smell of singed rubber. We manage to
put out the flames, but smoke still rises up through the
air, and here and there a red ember continues to glow
in the dark.

"We better get out of here," Pauly says.

I reach for Sarah. "Can you walk?"

She squeezes my hand as I pull her up. "It'll be
easier along the road than in the woods."

"She's right," I tell Pauly. "And we'll be able to
move faster, too."

We head out of the woods and toward the road. The
black, moonless sky is awash with bright, shimmering
stars. I slide my arm around Sarah's waist and she leans
on me, hardly able to put any weight on her left foot.
Our plastic-bag-covered bodies rub against each other.
I can tell by the way she winces and limps that this is
painful for her.

"Didn't know you were such a trouper," I tell her.

"Neither did I," she answers.

Headlights appear in the distance. We scamper into the ditch beside the road and hunker down. It seems like a long time before the car blows past. The road must be long and straight here; you can see headlights from miles away. Between Sarah's injured foot and the time we spend hiding from approaching cars, it's obvious we're not going to get very far tonight.

TWENTY-TWO

"Demerits will increase your stay at Lake Harmony."

When Sarah complains that it hurts too much to continue, we settle down in a cornfield.

"Know what's frickin' twisted?" Pauly asks as we lie on rough mats of broken cornstalks waiting for sleep. "My father would be proud of me now. It takes a real man to set fires and escape from boot camp."

"Maybe that's why he sent you," I speculate. "To see if you were man enough to escape."

Pauly chuckles bitterly. "How bent is that? Uh . . . ah-choo!" He sneezes. "Crap. And on top of everything else, I'm getting sick."

Sarah is lying close to me, her shoulder touching mine. I can feel her shivering. Without the plastic bags we'd probably be unbearably cold. With them, we're merely freezing. She's been quiet ever since we stopped.

"How's the foot?" I ask.

"Hurts."

"Bad?"

"Not too bad. More like a throbbing pain than a sharp one."

"Guess we'll stay here till the morning." Pauly starts to yawn, but it turns into a raspy cough. "Might as well try to get some sleep." He starts to nestle down between the stalks. The ground here is different from last night among the trees. The cornstalks are hard, and the air in the field is chillier than in the woods. I wonder how much sleep we'll really get before sunrise. But it's not long before Pauly's breathing is deep and rhythmic.

"I'm so cold," Sarah whispers.

I roll toward her, and she presses her back against my chest. Her hair is in my face.

"If I talk, will it keep you up?" she whispers.

"I'm not falling asleep anytime soon."

She nestles closer. "I'm scared, Garrett. What if we get caught?"

"They can't do anything worse to us than they've already done."

"What about the fire? That's arson, isn't it?"

"Oh, yeah. Guess they could do worse if they wanted to."

"You're not scared?"

"I don't know. Not sure I care anymore. Besides, in a weird way I like this. For the first time in months I actually feel alive. Being outside, going where I want, when I want, with no one telling me what to do. I don't know what's gonna happen next, but even if I get sent back, this may just have been worth it."

"You could be right," Sarah whispers. "After two and a half years in that place the thing I value more than anything is freedom."

She's quiet for a while. Just when I'm not sure she's still awake, she stirs. "Garrett?"

"Hmm?"

"Would you put your arm around me?"

"Sure."

I slide my arm over her shoulder and pull her closer, trying to share my body heat with her.

"Thanks," she whispers.

In the gray predawn I wake to Pauly coughing. A heavy wet fog has settled over the cornfield, and a film of water droplets covers our plastic-bag vests. Everything is damp and cold, and I'm shivering. Pauly's coughing fit ends, and he lies on the ground wheezing.

"You okay?" I ask.

"I'm sick," he croaks.

"It's freezing. My foot is killing me," Sarah whispers through chattering teeth.

No one budges. We lie curled up in the misty field, too cold and miserable to move.

"What are we gonna do?" Pauly asks after a while.

He's not asking how we'll get warm or find food. He's asking whether we should keep going or give up.

I don't dare to look at him. "What do you want to do?"

"Don't know," Pauly answers miserably.

And then through the haze comes a deep, resonating sound. I can almost feel the vibration through my skin.

"What's that?" Sarah asks.

"A foghorn," I answer. "From a boat. A really big boat like a tanker or something."

"The Saint Lawrence River!" Pauly exclaims, and props himself up on his elbow. "The border between the U.S. and Canada."

"We're *that* close?" Sarah asks.

"We must be," Pauly says with renewed energy.

Hope flows through us with the same warming effect as a cup of hot chocolate.

"There's got to be a bridge," Pauly says. "All those trucks must have gone over it. We just have to get across it and—" Before he can finish, he erupts into a spasm of coughing. Sarah gives me a concerned look.

"We gotta go," Pauly gasps once he's stopped coughing. "We didn't come this far not to."

Under the cover of fog we make our way through the tall brown stalks. The rows are planted north to south, which makes it easier for us. I've got my arm around Sarah, but she grimaces as she limps, and when Pauly stops to cough, he doubles over and his whole body trembles. Despite our Dumpster "feast" last night, my stomach is once again a knot of hunger.

The cornfield seems endless. As we trudge along, the fog around us turns lighter, and I realize the sun will rise soon. Every now and then the bellow of the foghorn rolls toward us. Meanwhile the mist keeps thinning and lifting, and the sun finally appears to our right like a ghostly circle, just a shade brighter than the haze around it. Pauly stops and points between the stalks. In the distance, through the thinning, drifting fog, we can see the rounded dark-green arc of a bridge.

The cornfield ends at a road, and from there we can see the span—long, narrow, and arched like a bow. But there's an unexpected obstacle. On the United States side is a brick building with a white sign that says in black letters U.S. CUSTOMS. Spanning the roadway leading to the bridge is a row of booths where cars must stop before they cross into Canada. They are customs inspection stations, and even at this early hour rows of vehicles are lined up waiting to go through each one.

"We can't go that way." Sarah is the first to voice what we've all just realized: With no identification or money they'll never let us across.

"What are we gonna do?" Pauly asks.

"Find another way," I reply. What other answer is there?

Across the road is a tall chain-link fence, like the one that surrounds Lake Harmony. Inside are several huge, windowless buildings covering an area as big as a couple of city blocks. From the long rows of docking bays and the trucks parked at some of them, I gather that it's some kind of truck depot or distribution center. Can we find a truck to hide in and ride through customs? Or maybe some unsuspecting employee I can chat up to see if there's another place to get across the river?

It's got to be worth a shot. The trucking operation appears to run around the clock. Even now at dawn a tractor-trailer trundles down the road, and the gates start to open automatically, no doubt triggered by some sort of sensor.

"Wait here," I tell Pauly and Sarah, and start to strip off my garbage-bag vest.

"Where are you going?" Sarah's voice rises nervously.

"I want to check that place out."

"Can't we come?" she asks anxiously.

I shake my head. "You can hardly walk, and everyone'll hear Pauly cough."

Sarah's forehead wrinkles with consternation. She doesn't want me to leave. But there's no other choice if we're going to find a way to Canada.

Across the road, the gates have swung open. I wait until the eighteen-wheeler goes through and then dash out of the cornfield and follow it in. With a soft whirring sound the gates close behind me. The truck heads toward the far end of one of the buildings. In the meantime I walk past the bays, each one sealed shut with a rolling metal garage-type door.

I walk the length of the building. By now the sun is firmly centered in the morning sky, and its rays warm my head and shoulders. At the end of the building I cross more asphalt, then walk through some low brown weeds and undergrowth toward the chain-link fence at the back of the property. The air feels cooler here.

Stopping at the fence, I curl my fingers through the cold metal links. On the other side, not more than two hundred yards away, is the broadest river I have ever seen. The water is dark gray-green, and in the near distance is a vast channel. Beyond that are small, tree-covered islands. Some have houses on them. Past those islands is a distant shore with more houses. And that, I assume, is Canada.

If we can just find a way across . . .

Turning from the fence, I start to walk along the shady side of the huge building. I'm not sure what I'm looking for. A miracle? A friendly face who'll tell me exactly how my friends and I can cross the border?

I pass endless truck bays, not a soul in sight. No, wait. Down at the far end of the building, where the sunlight cuts a wide swath, two people are standing, talking. One of them looks familiar.

Just at that moment Rebecca turns her head in my direction.

TWENTY-THREE

"You will report any infraction of the rules immediately."

"Hey!" She starts to run toward me.

I take off for the back of the next building. It's a race, only there's no finish line in sight. I'm running purely on the hope that somewhere I'll find a way through the fence. The good news is that thanks to all the running I did at Lake Harmony, I'm in pretty good shape. The bad news is that lack of food and sleep has sapped my strength, and I quickly start to feel it.

Over my shoulder, I see that Rebecca is about fifty yards behind, fists clenched, arms pumping.

I run behind the second building, searching the

chain-link fence for a gate or an opening. Anything to get out of this place. In the flip-flops, my feet slap the asphalt painfully. I can feel every rock and pebble through the soles.

Finding only an endless high fence behind the second building, I race toward the third. Rebecca is still behind me. But unless she's a marathon runner, she must be feeling the strain too. There are no openings in the fence behind the third building either. So I head for the next. This trucking center is huge, but I can't keep up this pace. My heart is pounding, my lungs are burning, and my feet are killing me. Rebecca is still behind me, but I can see by the way her arms flail that she's starting to weaken.

A painful stitch develops in my side, and my legs are starting to cramp, but I have to keep going. I didn't come all this way to give up now. And I'm not going back to Lake Harmony.

Rebecca and I both slow to a limping trot. Maybe she's cramping too. We pass behind the fourth building and head for the fifth. The pain is gruesome, almost unbearable. But in a strange way my experience at Lake Harmony helps me here, too—I've learned to cope with a level of pain I never knew I could tolerate.

We slow to a jog. It's almost laughable. Pretty soon we'll both be on our knees, crawling. I keep an eye on her. If she speeds up, I speed up. If she slows down, I do the same. Meanwhile, I'm still searching for that way out.

We get around the fifth building. The asphalt is littered with shreds of cardboard boxes, cigarette butts, broken liquor bottles, empty beer cans, and busted wooden pallets. Looks like there isn't much trucking activity here. It's more like a place where teenagers gather at night to drink and hang out.

But if that's what they do, they're probably not coming in the front gate. So how do they get in?

The answer is a patch of smooth, bare dirt where the bottom of the fence curls up just enough for someone to slither under. Piled on the other side are big black metal drums, the kind you see on the news when they've discovered some illegal chemical dumping ground. Suddenly, as if she's read my mind, Rebecca starts to run harder.

I go as fast as I can, knowing I need to get under the fence before she gets there. When I reach it I practically dive onto my stomach and start to crawl, but halfway under, the back of my shirt catches. I don't care about tearing it, but I'm caught and can't go any further. *Damn it!* I have to back out and start again. Rebecca is only twenty yards away now. This time I start to slide under the fence on my back, so if my clothes get caught, I'll be able to unsnag them.

I'm halfway under when Rebecca grabs one of my ankles. I kick my foot loose, and when she grabs for it again, I plant my other foot against her chest and push as hard as I can.

Rebecca flies backward and hits the ground hard. In the meantime I manage to get under the fence. But once I'm on the other side, relief and fatigue settle over me like a heavy shawl. Suddenly I'm too tired to even get to my feet.

Meanwhile Rebecca sits up on the asphalt and rubs her elbow where she must have banged it against the ground. We're both breathing hard.

"You okay?" I ask through the fence.

"What do you care?" she snaps.

"I didn't mean to hurt you."

She gives me a hard look. "Shouldn't you be running away?"

"Probably."

"So why aren't you?"

The answer is that I'm tired and for the moment, with the fence separating us, I don't have to. But I'm not about to tell her that. Besides, there's something I'd like to know: "Why are you doing this?"

"What?" She looks at me like I'm crazy.

"Why are you chasing me? Why do you work as a transporter?"

Rebecca frowns. "It's my job."

"But you were once at Lake Harmony."

She blinks with surprise. "How do you know that?"

"You told me. Well, not you. Harry did. About eight months ago. We were all in a car together."

Rebecca slides her eyes off to the side as if trying to remember.

"He called me blue blood," I remind her.

She shrugs. "So?"

"I don't get it," I tell her. "You've been there. You know what it's like."

"And your point is?"

"How can you help send other kids there?"

"Maybe they deserve it," she says.

"Did you?"

"Matter of fact, I probably did."

"Why?"

She gives me an exasperated look. "What do you care?"

"I just want to understand."

"You want to understand? Stay there and I'll be glad to tell you." She slowly rises to her feet and limps toward the fence. Looks like she must have gotten a cramp or pulled a muscle chasing me. At the same time I also get up and roll one of the big metal drums until it blocks the smooth spot where the fence curls inward. Then I roll a few more drums in tight against it so she can't crawl under and push the first one out of the way.

Rebecca glares at me through the chain links. "Sooner or later you're going back. And when you do, you're going to be sorry."

"Why are you so angry?" I ask.

"Because I'm in pain, okay? I'm pissed off that you made me chase you. Besides, haven't you heard? Everyone who goes through boot camp has anger issues."

"I don't."

She starts to shake her head dismissively, then stops and looks at me again. "Blue blood. I remember. You were a strange one."

"Why?"

"You just were."

"Maybe because I didn't deserve to go."

"That's what everyone thinks."

"Doesn't mean a few of them aren't right."

Rebecca takes a deep breath and lets it out slowly. She rubs her thigh where the cramp or pull must be. "You shouldn't be talking to me. You should be running as fast as you can."

"Harry wouldn't be happy to hear you say that."

"Don't you know what's going to happen if you get caught?"

"You'll take me back. They'll put me in TI and beat me every few days. Sooner or later they'll manage to rewire my brain so I believe I really did deserve to be sent there and that they saved my life and I probably would have died otherwise."

Rebecca rolls her eyes, then reaches into her pocket and takes out a pack of cigarettes. She lights one and takes a deep drag. She glances at me. "Want one?"

"No, thanks."

"Never smoked?"

I shake my head. Rebecca takes another deep drag. "Well, thanks for not reminding me that I could probably run faster if I didn't."

"My pleasure."

She gives me a funny look. "You're the one whose parents sent you away because you wouldn't stop seeing some older woman. Your teacher, right?"

"Some crime, huh? And Harry told you not to believe a word I said. He said I was a brilliant manipulator."

"That's what he always says."

"What do *you* think?"

"I think it's mostly true."

"Mostly, but not always. Only he said it's not your job to decide."

"That about sums it up."

"Just following orders."

"Everyone follows orders. You can't keep a job if you don't. You either wind up in the street or in jail."

"The Nazis were just following Hitler's orders."

Rebecca squints suspiciously. "Maybe Harry was right about you, Mr. Brilliant Manipulator."

Am I wasting time talking to her? Shouldn't I get out of here before Harry shows up? But before I go, I have to try something. "Look, my life is in your hands. Just because Harry has decided it's not his job to question orders, does that mean you have to be the same way? Or does the very fact that I'm asking mean I'm trying to manipulate you?"

"Maybe."

"What if 'manipulate' is the wrong word? What if I'm trying to persuade you on an issue you're uncertain about? Is that wrong? What if it's something I really believe in, but you haven't yet made up your mind? How is that manipulation?"

Rebecca doesn't answer. She blows some smoke and looks off in the distance as if thinking. Finally she drops the cigarette and crushes it beneath her shoe. Then she gives me an intense, focused look. "You know, it's not just you we're after. It's the other two as well. Maybe everything you've said is true for you. That doesn't mean it's true for them."

"It's true for them, too. Otherwise I wouldn't be with them."

She gives me a dubious look. "You better get going. Harry catches me talking to you, it's not going to do either of us any good."

I take a few steps back. "But it's your job."

"Harry says one thing about this business: There's a never-ending supply. If we lose you, we'll just be sent to grab someone else. Now get."

I back away. Rebecca just stands there. I keep backing away. She still hasn't moved. I turn and run.

Walking quickly through the woods. I need to get to Pauly and Sarah, but I can't go straight back. Rebecca knows the direction I left in. Maybe she let me go on purpose, hoping that I'd lead Harry and her to Pauly and Sarah. Damn it! When she mentioned Pauly and Sarah, I should have pretended that we'd separated right after leaving Lake Harmony and that I had no idea where they'd gone. Now she knows they're around here somewhere.

The woods end at a narrow road that follows the shoreline. The road is lined with small resorts, motels, stores, and restaurants, many of them featuring rustic log-cabin designs. They have names like Riverside Rest, Riverview, Waterline Café, and Don's Daily Boat Rentals.

Wait a minute...boat rentals? That could be our shot.

A couple of hours pass before I get back to the cornfield. I've taken the most circuitous route possible to avoid being seen or followed. Pauly and Sarah are huddled on the ground in their plastic-bag vests. The sight of them is shocking. Somehow in the past few hours I forgot how haggard and dirty we are. In addition Pauly and Sarah look pale and sickly.

Still, Sarah smiles happily when I appear. Pauly looks glassy-eyed and feverish but asks, "Where have you been?"

"Almost got caught." I tell them about Rebecca. "So they know we're here, and they're looking for us."

"Crap," Pauly mutters.

The sun is higher now, almost overhead, and here among the dead brown cornstalks, without a breeze, it almost feels warm. Pauly's forehead glistens with perspiration, but it can't be from the sun's heat. He must have a fever.

"I think we have a chance," I tell them. "There's a place down the road that rents boats."

Both Sarah and Pauly give me puzzled looks. "We're . . . gonna rent a boat?"

"No. We're gonna steal one."

We head into the woods. It's slow going. Sarah's foot is swollen and tender, and I have to support her. Pauly stops often and coughs, his thin body shuddering with each hack. Each time he coughs, Sarah and I exchange nervous looks. If Harry and Rebecca are anywhere near, they'll be certain to hear him.

I lead them to the spot where the trees end at the narrow road. From here we can see the rustic motels and the run-down brown shack behind the sign for Don's Daily Boat Rentals.

"That place?" Pauly whispers hoarsely.

"Yeah."

"So what are we waiting for?" Sarah asks, eager to get going.

"That pickup wasn't there before," I explain. A dented light-blue pickup truck is parked next to the shack.

"What do we do?" Sarah asks.

"Let's see what happens."

We wait, hidden in the trees. Now and then a car rattles past, usually an older model, sometimes with rusted-out lower panels. It's well past summer-vacation season, and cars pass at a leisurely pace, as if no one is in a rush to go anywhere.

When a shiny new maroon sedan comes down the road, I do a double-take. The driver is wearing a cowboy hat and craning his head this way and that. Reflexively I duck down even further than before.

"Was it them?" Sarah whispers.

"One of them. Maybe both. I didn't get a good look."

"What do we do now?" Pauly asks.

If Harry and Rebecca just passed, hopefully it will be a while before they come back this way. Now the sound of a sputtering engine catches my attention. Across the road, exhaust spits out of the light-blue pickup. It starts to back up, and heads away down the road.

This might be our only chance.

"Ready?" I ask.

Pauly bites his lip, his eyes darting back and forth. But Sarah is already pushing herself up. "Let's do it."

I slide my arm under her shoulder, and we step out of the woods.

And into trouble.

TWENTY-FOUR

"Additional privileges will be your reward for rising through the levels."

Two hundred yards to our left, just where the road begins to curve around a bend, the shiny new maroon sedan is parked in front of a small yellow house with black shutters. A woman in jeans and a man in a cowboy hat are standing at the front door as if waiting for someone to answer the doorbell. The woman sees us and points. The man in the cowboy hat quickly turns his head.

Pauly sprints away. I more or less pick up Sarah and follow. We dash past the sign for Don's Daily Boat Rentals and around the brown wooden shack.

Beyond it is a short green lawn, then a rickety wooden dock sticking out into the river with four dented old aluminum skiffs tied to it.

The dock bobs and wobbles unsteadily as we run onto it. Each skiff is about fifteen feet long with three bench seats and a small black outboard on the stern.

"You know how to drive one of these?" Pauly asks.

"Used to," I answer as I help Sarah down into the middle seat of the last boat. The red plastic gas can reads full. I pump the black plastic ball, open the choke, and give the pull cord a good yank. The engine comes to life and revs with a cloud of white smoke. But before we go, I have an idea and climb up onto the dock.

"Pauly, quick." I jump down into the boat behind ours. In the stern gunnel is a screw stopper for draining the boat when it's in dry dock. I start to undo it. "See what I'm doing?" I hold up the stopper, then toss it into the water.

"Yeah." Pauly moves down to the next boat and does the same. I leapfrog him and do the third boat. Cold water seeps through the holes and into the bottoms of the boats.

"Way to—," Paul starts to give a little cheer as we climb back into the first boat with Sarah in it, but he freezes with his mouth open. I twist around and see why. Harry is barreling around the shack at full speed. Rebecca follows, hobbling.

"Untie the bow!" I yell.

Pauly knows what to do. I twist the throttle wide open, and the outboard engine whines as the bow lifts and we start to accelerate away. Behind us the dock rises and drops under Harry's heavy footsteps, but there's no way he's going to catch us now.

The dock grows smaller as we head out into the river. Harry stands at the end with his hands on his hips and a furious expression on his face. Rebecca is next to him with her arms crossed. We watch them from the boat for a few moments, unsure whether to let ourselves feel the elation of escape. But Harry and Rebecca just stand there. As incredible as it seems, we've done it!

In the boat, Pauly turns and faces forward, taking the wind in his face, his plastic-bag vest rattling in the breeze. The river must be at least a mile wide. The far shore looks green and forested with houses set among the trees. The water has a slight chop, and as the boat gains speed, it begins to bang and bounce, kicking up white wings of spray on either side. Huddled on the middle seat, Sarah faces me with her back to the wind, the edges of her plastic-bag vest rippling, her head bobbing every time we bounce off a wave. For the first time in hours she smiles. Her lips move, but her voice is lost in the wind and engine noise.

I point to my ear. "Can't hear you. Talk louder!"

"I said, pretty good for a city boy!" she yells. But the words have hardly left her lips when the smile is replaced by widened eyes and a jaw dropping in surprise as she stares past me back toward shore. Harry and Rebecca have jumped into one of the other rental boats, and Harry yanks on the starter cord while Rebecca unties the bow rope. A puff of white smoke rises behind them as they leave the dock in pursuit.

Sensing that something is wrong, Pauly swivels his head and looks. His lips move. The words are lost in the wind, but I think he's just said, "They're gonna sink."

Harry must be so intent on chasing us that he didn't notice that the stopper was gone. There's almost always a little rain collected in the bottom of these boats, so the water inside probably didn't even register in his mind. By now we're a quarter of a mile out in the river, leaving an ever-broadening white wake. The Canadian shore is three quarters of a mile away. It's hard to imagine Harry and Rebecca will make it that far.

Sarah gives me a concerned look. These boats have no cushions or life preservers. And the river water is cold. Even if they know how to swim, they'll probably succumb to hypothermia before they can reach safety.

Pauly's face goes somber as he figures it out too. Is our freedom worth two lives? But if we go back to warn them, we might get caught. The Canadian side is getting closer. Now I can see the windows in the houses and a car driving along a road.

Pauly and Sarah continue to stare back. Three hundred yards behind us Harry's boat bangs and splashes over the waves, kicking plumes of spray from both sides. Did Harry notice the stopper was out and stuff a rag in its place?

By now we're almost halfway across. Individual trees are beginning to come into focus. Behind us, Harry's boat is no longer bouncing over the waves. It sits deeper now, pushing water ahead of it like a tugboat.

Pauly and Sarah study me as if waiting for my decision.

You didn't go through all that pain and suffering and come all this way to turn back now.

If the places were reversed, there's no way Harry would come back and save you.

But you can't let people die.

Can you?

Our skiff bangs over the waves. The opposite shore is getting close. I can see each tree clearly, boats, docks, a bright yellow kayak pulled up on a lawn.

Well behind us, Harry's boat is low in the water, hardly moving anymore.

Ahead of us are several resorts with docks. I head for one where the windows appear to be boarded up for winter. Now, instead of giving me searching looks, both Pauly and Sarah look away. As if neither can meet my gaze.

Moments later I slow down and ease the boat beside a dock, then reach over the gunnel and steady it so Pauly can help Sarah climb out. Sarah glances toward the boarded-up resort and then—sensing that something isn't right—turns to look at the idling outboard motor, and then at me. "Aren't you coming?"

I shake my head.

Standing beside her on the dock, Pauly purses his lips, then nods as if he understands. Sarah blinks, fighting off tears. "It's not fair."

Out in the middle of the river Harry's boat is no longer moving. Instead it sits almost level with the water.

"I better go."

"You're a good guy," Pauly says glumly.

Tears start to fall from Sarah's eyes. She kneels down on the dock, takes my face in her hands, and kisses me on the lips. "Thank you."

"Say hello to your aunt for me," I tell her.

Sarah glances at Pauly, who lowers his gaze and looks away. She turns back to me, her dark eyes glistening wet. "Garrett . . . there is no aunt."

"Huh?" I don't get it.

She takes my hand and squeezes it. "There's an aunt in Minnesota, but we made up the one in Toronto." She wipes a tear from her cheek. "We were afraid if we said we didn't know anyone in Canada, you wouldn't help us. You'd think it was hopeless."

I'm stunned. *Of all the people . . .* I never thought they'd lie to me.

"Then what are you gonna do?" I ask.

"Try to make it on our own," Pauly says. "No matter what, the American authorities can't get us here. Listen, Garrett, we had to do it. We would have died in that place."

Brilliant manipulators. Strangely I don't feel angry. I almost admire them. They were desperate. I can't blame them, because like me they didn't belong at Lake Harmony.

"Try to understand," Sarah pleads.

"I understand." I push the boat away from the dock and turn it around.

Believe me, I understand . . .

By the time I get back out to the middle of the river, Harry's boat is swamped. He and Rebecca are sitting on the bench seats, holding on to the gunnels, the cold river water up to their waists, watching me with silent expressions. Rebecca's teeth are chattering, her lips are blue, and her jaw is trembling uncontrollably. I stop my boat about thirty feet away.

"Come back to watch us drown?" Harry snarls through clenched teeth, as if he refuses to let me see how cold he is.

"Not my thing," I answer.

"Then what do you want?"

"If I save you, promise you'll take me back to the Canadian side."

"I'd rather drown," Harry answers.

"For God's sake, Harry," Rebecca blurts.

"You go with him; I'll stay here," Harry says belligerently.

"What's the big deal?" I ask. "So what if three of us get away? Aren't you the one who said that the great thing about this business is there's a never-ending supply?"

Harry stares angrily at Rebecca, as if he knows where those words came from. She hangs her head. Just then three big air bubbles break the surface behind them, and the stern of their skiff starts to sink. The nose tips skyward, and Rebecca screams. I move my boat closer, kill the engine, and reach over the side to help her. The skiff rocks as she climbs in and flops onto the seat. She's soaked, dripping from the chest down, and shivering from the cold. Just as his boat begins to slide backward and disappear beneath the surface, Harry leaps forward and with a splash grabs the gunnel of my skiff, nearly tipping it over. Once the boat steadies, Rebecca and I pull him in.

A moment later they're sitting on the center bench, dripping wet, teeth chattering behind blue lips. Harry's lost his cowboy hat. He pulls off his cowboy boots and about a quart of water pours out of each one. I climb back to the stern and grab the pull cord to restart the engine.

"I'm going to Canada," I tell Harry. "And you're going to let me go when I get there."

He grits his teeth and looks like he wants to kill. But then his eyes relax and his mouth softens into a smile as he looks past me. The distant wail of a siren cuts through the air. A black and white speedboat is racing toward us with red lights flashing. It's kicking up a white plume six feet high and leaving a broad wake. A police boat.

TWENTY-FIVE

"You must demonstrate your allegiance to Lake Harmony's program."

As I look longingly toward the Canadian shore and try to judge the distance, a heavy dose of disappointment weighs down my shoulders. There's no way I'll get there. That police boat is ten times faster than this old aluminum skiff. In no time it pulls within a dozen yards of us. There are three officers aboard, all wearing black bulletproof vests. The younger two prop M19s on their hips. The older officer, probably the captain of the boat, holds a cocked forty-five-caliber semi-automatic. These guys mean business.

"Hands on your heads," the captain orders. "You take that boat without permission?"

The answer is obvious.

"What's the story?" the captain asks.

"The young lady and I are bounty hunters," Harry reports with forced calmness. "We work for Lake Harmony, a school that specializes in—"

"I know what Lake Harmony is." The captain cuts him short.

"We were hired to apprehend this young man and bring him back."

"Then why is he driving the boat?" the captain asks.

Harry goes into his folksy, friendly act. "With all due respect, sir, the young lady and I are awful cold. If you'd like to bring us in, I'll be glad to explain."

At the police station it takes hours to straighten things out. Don, the owner of the boat, has arrived. He's a large man with a deep, bellowing voice like a bull's. His demands for restitution for the skiff that sank reverberate through the building. A lot of phone calls go back and forth between the police and Lake Harmony and between Harry and Lake Harmony.

At one point, while Harry and the police are in an office on a speakerphone to Lake Harmony, Rebecca and I are left alone on a wooden bench in the hall. My flip-flops are gone; my feet are bare. They've given Rebecca a pair of gray sweatpants and a navy-blue hoodie with ALEXANDRIA BAY PD printed in white letters.

"Nice outfit. Think you'll get to keep it?" I ask.

Rebecca shakes her head. "My stuff is in the laundry room drying. Soon as it's ready, I'll have to give these things back."

"Too bad. It could be a souvenir, you know?"

We share a smile. Rebecca tugs at the drawstring on the sweatshirt's hood. "Can I ask you a question? Why did you do it? You could have gotten away."

"You and Harry would have died."

A telephone rings somewhere. Two police officers come down the hall carrying cardboard Pizza Hut boxes. Neither one looks at Rebecca or me. The smell of the pizza reminds me of how long it's been since I ate a real meal.

"Do you know what's going to happen when you go back?" Rebecca asks.

I slowly nod my head yes.

Rebecca turns away and doesn't look at me again.

It's close to midnight when we finally leave the police station. A thin crescent moon hangs in the black sky. The ground is icy under my bare feet.

"Turn around," Harry orders.

"Why?" I ask.

The answer is his hand on my shoulder, roughly spinning me. He yanks my arms behind my back, and I feel hard metal handcuffs close around my wrists. I guess since I wasn't formally charged with a crime, the police didn't feel the need to restrain me. But out here in the cold night air it's a different story. Holding my arm, Harry leads me to the rental car and shoves me into the back, then slams the door.

As we drive through the dark, I wonder where Pauly and Sarah are. I'd like to think they've found a friendly, sympathetic doctor who's taken them in and fixed their ailments. I picture them huddled in warm wool blankets, sitting at an old wooden table feasting on steaming bowls of hearty soup and recounting the incredible story of their escape. It would make a nice movie. There's a happy ending, the good guys get away . . . well, two out of three good guys, at least.

Harry looks in the rearview mirror and sees the twisted smirk on my face. "What's so funny?"

"I don't know. The irony, I guess."

"What irony?"

"That I'm here all over again," I explain. "In the backseat of a car with you guys. My hands cuffed behind my back and going numb. Needing to use the bathroom and knowing you'll never believe me. It's like nothing's changed."

"Just wait till you get back to Lake Harmony, partner. Plenty's gonna change for you," Harry says ominously. Rebecca looks over the seat at me, then turns to Harry. "Are you sure we're doing the right thing?"

"Don't start that again."

"He saved us."

"Lucky for us and too bad for him."

"You know it's not right."

Harry doesn't answer. We ride in silence down the straight, dark, two-lane road, the endless stream of yellow dashes disappearing in front of us.

It's the middle of the night when we return to Lake Harmony. Harry drives through the front gate and up to the administration building. While he's parking the car, Joe and the troll come down the steps. Without saying hello to Harry or Rebecca, Joe opens the back door, reaches in, and yanks me out.

"Welcome home," he growls, and punches me in the stomach as hard as he can.

TWENTY-SIX

"Success at Lake Harmony requires renouncing your former life."

"We believe she's in Canada." I'm facedown on the wooden floor in the lobby of the administration building when I hear these words come through the closed door of Mr. Z's office. "No, that would be considered crossing international boundaries for the purpose of kidnapping, Mr. Sundwald. No, no, that was different. Let me explain. You may remember that you gave us written permission to enter your house and take Sarah. We can't do that now. Canadian law prevents it."

The wooden floor smells lemony. My hands are still cuffed behind my back. A few feet away, Joe and the

troll sit in chairs. My stomach is sore from the punch
Joe delivered. Mr. Z's voice continues through the
door.

"I'm sorry, Mr. Sundwald, but our hands are tied
by law. Yes, she was here a long time. We did the best
we could. Some children resist more than others. No,
if you read the contract, you'll see that it clearly states
that we can't be held responsible for her actions. It was
her decision to escape. Well, I can't stop you from doing
that, but you'll discover that our contract holds up very
well in court. If that's your decision, Mr. Sundwald.
Good-bye."

The crash of the telephone comes in unexpectedly
sharp contrast to the calm tone of Mr. Z's voice while
he spoke to Sarah's father. A torrent of curses follows.
Chair legs scrape against the floor. The office door
swings open, and I see a pair of black shoes and the
cuffs of gray slacks.

"Well, well, if it isn't our very own Harry
Houdini." The bottom of a shoe presses down slowly
and painfully on the back of my neck. "You've been a
very bad boy, Garrett. I imagine you think you're some
kind of hero, but you're about to learn that no good
deed goes unpunished."

The pressure on my neck continues to build until it
feels like my spinal cord might snap. Despite my best
efforts not to, I squirm, and a groan of agony escapes
my lips. "You are a first, Garrett. Until you and your
friends, no resident has ever left Lake Harmony without
permission for longer than a few hours. Certainly
never for as long as a day. Not only have you changed

that, but it appears that your friends may never return. Paul Vetare is in a hospital in Toronto. It seems that his parents are so concerned about his physical condition that they've decided against having him come back here. Sarah Sundwald has disappeared."

Mr. Z's shoe presses down even harder. The pain is hideous. "Please, sir," I hear myself beg. "Stop."

"Feeling uncomfortable, Garrett?" Mr. Z asks, almost sadistically. "Believe me, this is nothing compared to what you're in for. You've created a real problem for us. Not only with the parents of Sarah Sundwald and Paul Vetare, but with the rest of our residents as well. Clearly, for something like this to occur, there must be an unacceptable level of defiance throughout the entire resident population. The only way to deal with a situation like this will be on a global scale."

The sole of his shoe crushes down even harder. I squirm and beg him again to stop. Finally he does, and says to Joe and the troll, "Take him to TI. You know what to do."

I am beaten on and off for the next twenty-four hours. The rule against leaving visible marks is temporarily suspended. My lips are swollen and split, my eyes blackened, my nose raw from bleeding.

"Time to eat. Let's go, smart guy," Joe finally says. Bloodied, bruised, exhausted, I start to rise.

Smack! He slaps me hard in the face. "Did I tell you to stand?"

How else can I go to the food hall?

"On your hands and knees," he orders.

With Joe following, I crawl into the food hall.

"Good dental hygiene protects more than your teeth," an RL blares. *"Recent studies suggest a link between oral inflammation due to bacteria and clogged arteries and blood clots . . . "*

No one is listening. They're all staring at me. Now I understand why the rule against leaving marks was ignored. They want everyone to see what I look like. I am a warning in case anyone else is entertaining ideas of escape.

Joe makes me crawl all the way to the Dignity table, where Adam grins with delight at my return.

"Daily brushing and flossing ensure your teeth will last a lifetime—"

The RL stops abruptly. Some brief, loud static pierces the air, and then Mr. Z gets on the public-address system: "As you all know, we recently had a major breach of security here at Lake Harmony. Rules were broken, facilities were damaged, and in the process there were numerous attempts by residents to leave the grounds without permission. After considering the situation, I have come to the conclusion that stern measures must be taken to guarantee nothing like this ever happens again. I also believe that while certain of the guilty parties have been identified and severely punished, it will be impossible to know for sure who else may have participated. Therefore I have decided that the entire resident body must bear the responsibility. As of this moment, every resident will be immediately demoted one entire level."

A collective groan rises from the food hall, but it is immediately silenced by shouts of "Shut up!" from the "mothers," "fathers," and chaperones. The crowd quiets, and the motivational tape resumes: *"An added benefit of good dental hygiene is clean, fresh-smelling breath . . . "*

But the drone of the tape isn't punctuated by the usual dining sounds of spoons on plates. All around the food hall kids are staring with frowns, sneers, and other angry expressions—at me.

The first attack comes during study. I'm sitting in a carrel when Adam, Unibrow Robert, and David Zitface pass. A bolt of stabbing pain shoots up my left arm. I yank the thing out. It's the handle of a plastic spoon scraped down into a needle-sharp point, now red with blood.

The next attack comes when we line up for lunch. A sharp kick to the back of my leg makes my knee buckle, and I fall. By the time I get up, it's impossible to tell where the kick came from. It could have been any of half a dozen kids. Joe is standing a few feet away. Our eyes meet, and the slightest smile flits across his lips. He knows who did it.

At lunch, while the staff patrol the aisles between other tables, someone smacks my head from behind hard enough to knock me sideways. The blow leaves me dazed. None of the staff seem to have noticed.

The attacks continue throughout the day. Frequent and without warning. By dinnertime I'm on edge, paranoid, constantly looking over my shoulder, never knowing where the next blow will come from. By Shut Down I'm totally exhausted. In the past four days I've probably gotten less than twelve hours' sleep total. I can hardly keep my eyes open as we march down the hall toward the dorm.

"Garrett, step out," Joe barks.

Now what? my sleep-deprived brain wonders.

"Come with me," he orders, while the troll leads the rest of Dignity into the dorm. In a daze I follow Joe down the hall. He pushes through a door to the outside. The air is crisp and cold, the grass stiff under my bare feet. I brace myself for another beating.

"I hear you like spending the night outside, smart guy," Joe says.

I'm too tired to search for the hidden meaning behind this statement.

"Don't move." Joe bends down behind me. Something hard and cold clamps around my ankle, followed by a loud, metallic click. I look down and see that I've been chained to a stake.

TWENTY-SEVEN

"You must demonstrate your loyalty by policing fellow residents."

I spend the night curled up on the cold ground, trembling and unable to sleep for more than a few moments at a time.

"Wake up," someone says.

I open my eyes from a brief, shivering dream. Joe is standing over me wearing a dark-green down vest over a gray hoodie. White mist escapes his lips when he exhales. I'm shaking uncontrollably, and my teeth chatter with such force, I fear they'll chip. I've never been this cold in my life. Joe crouches down and unlocks the shackle from my ankle.

"Get up."

Trembling, I slowly try to rise, but my legs are stiff, and it's difficult to find my balance. *Wham!* Before I've even straightened up, Joe smacks me on the side of the head and I tumble back to the ground.

"Get up," he snarls.

Dizzy and dazed, I try again. But before I can get to my feet, he hits me.

"Get up."

My head throbs and feels like it's going to explode. I try to rise, then lose my balance and fall.

"Get up!" Joe shouts.

But I can't. Not because I don't want to follow orders, but because I'm too dizzy.

"I said, get up!" Joe shouts.

I manage to get to my hands and knees. Joe kicks me in the stomach and I roll over, gasping for breath.

"Get up!"

What's the point?

"I said, get up!" Joe shouts.

I curl into a ball and remain on the cold ground, shivering and cowering, waiting for the next blow.

"Bet you wish you'd never gone back to save those transporters, huh, smart guy?" Joe taunts. "How stupid was that? You could be free right now. Instead you had to be a hero."

On the ground, eyes squeezed tight, body tense, I wait for the next blow, only it doesn't come. Instead I hear something snap. Joe has gone over to a tree and broken off a long, thin branch.

"Know what the word 'breakage' means, smart

guy?" Joe asks, scraping the twigs and dead leaves off the branch. *Whap!* He whips the stick against the bottoms of my bare feet. The sudden, searing pain makes me cry out and curl my toes. But balled up on the ground like that, there's no way I can protect my feet.

"In case they didn't teach you in your fancy private school, allow me to explain." *Whap! Whap!* He whips the stick down again and again. "In business, manufacturers know that any time they ship a product, a few pieces are going to be damaged on the way. That's breakage."

Whap! "In every crate of eggs, one or two will break. Same with every truckload of bottled beer, and every train car filled with cattle. There's always going to be some breakage." *Whap!*

"By now you've probably figured out where I'm going with this. Here at Lake Harmony we expect some breakage too. Not every resident who comes here gets to go home. Despite our best efforts it just seems to happen every now and then."

Whap!

Later they make me run barefoot, carrying a car tire in each arm. If I drop a tire, they hit me. If I trip and fall, they hit me. My feet go numb with pain. Finally, when I can't take another step and even the blows can't make me get up, they make me crawl to TI, where they cuff my hands behind my back. In my exhausted state I actually welcome the thought of being able to lie down, even if it's with my face on the floor.

Adam and the troll are waiting for me. Adam shouts, "Kneel!"

"Huh?" I'm so tired and dazed, I don't understand.

"You heard me."

"But . . ."

"I said, kneel!" Adam yells. I drop to my knees. My eyes are so heavy with exhaustion that it's impossible to keep them open.

"Open your eyes!" Adam orders.

I try, but I can only get them partway open before the heaviness begins to force them back down again.

Smack! Adam hits my face with an open hand.

"Good, Adam," the troll says. "You're on your way back to Level Five."

"Thank you, sir."

The sting of Adam's slap becomes a hot, fading memory, gradually replaced by the overpowering drowsiness. My eyes start to droop again.

Smack! "Wake up, you piece of crap!" Adam shouts. "No one said you could close your eyes."

The troll leaves Adam with orders to not let me sleep. He slaps my face, stamps on my bare feet, pinches and pokes. But despite all that, I often drift off into a kneeling dream state the second the pain stops.

The door opens, and Mr. Sparks comes in carrying a paper plate with a sandwich. Adam removes the handcuffs, and I reach up, but the plate falls out of my hands. The bread separates and a few thin slices of mystery meat flop onto the floor. Adam starts to say something about that being my tough luck, but my eyes are already closing.

I think I hear Mr. Sparks telling Adam to take a

break and get some lunch, but maybe I've dreamed it. Did I hear the door open and close, or was that a dream, too? I could open my eyes to look, but it takes more energy than I can muster.

"Garrett?"

At the sensation of a hand on my shoulder, I shrink back in anticipation of pain. But the hand doesn't squeeze or pinch or poke.

"You can lie down."

I open my eyes and see Mr. Sparks's face.

"Go on." He presses down gently. "No one's going to hurt you."

I lie down.

Voices.

"Why's he lying down, sir?"

"He passed out."

"But sir, Joe said he's not supposed to sleep."

"He passed out. What was I supposed to do?"

"Did you try to wake him, sir?"

"What do you think?"

"Sir, if Joe finds him like this, I'll get demerits."

I feel the toe of a shoe prod me. "Hey, wake up."

It's going to take a lot more than that.

"Get up!" Adam screams at me.

I raise my head and look pleadingly at Mr. Sparks.

"Unnh!" A jolt of pain leaves me gasping as Adam delivers a kick to my ribs. Mr. Sparks winces sympathetically, but there's nothing he can do.

TWENTY-EIGHT

**"You will be deemed ready to leave Lake Harmony
when you have expressed gratitude to your parents
for sending you here."**

It was stupid of me to try to
escape. I was wrong to help Sarah
and Paul escape. I was sent here
because I was disrespectful and
ignorant. I was disobedient and
out of control. I've grown up a lot.
I hardly even think about Sabrina
anymore. I think I'm ready to
go home and be respectful to my

parents. But that will be up to my father, Joe, to decide.

"That's good, Garrett." At the touch of Joe's hand, I cower and jerk away. We're in Reflections, and I've just written in my notebook.

"Hey, come on." My family "father" reaches out and pats my shoulder with approval. "We're past all that now, right?"

"I—I guess, sir." I glance furtively at the other members of my family, but no one is paying attention. Weeks have passed since the escape. Most of my bruises have healed; most of the black-and-blue marks have disappeared. All that was part of the old Garrett. They don't attack me anymore. These days I'm just another quiet, obedient kid working his way up the levels. Even Adam doesn't seem interested in me. He's a Level Six now and hardly says anything or looks at anyone. Joe says he'll probably graduate soon.

I'm getting close to Level Five myself. Joe says I'm progressing really fast. He says sometimes the kids who've resisted the most change the fastest once they've learned their lesson. I understand what he means. At sixteen we think we know everything, but the truth is we're too young and immature to really know anything. Like yesterday I had to report a Level One for whispering at lunch, but he should have known better. If he ever wants to be more than a minimum-wager, he's going to have to shape up.

There are new kids in Dignity. Kids with anger

issues, who smirk and roll their eyes and think they're smart and can get away with stuff. Last night after Shut Down, Unibrow Robert, David Zitface, and Babyface Miles beat up a kid in the bathroom. We all heard it, but the troll said if any of us wanted to graduate from Lake Harmony, we'd better pretend we didn't hear anything. Unibrow Robert is the new enforcer now. At mealtime if he wants my fries, I always give them to him. What difference does it make? Like the RLs say, they're not even good for you.

Mr. Sparks is my favorite chaperone. Whenever he sees me, he says: "How's it going, Garrett?" I always answer: "Just staying out of trouble, sir." Sometimes when I say that, he looks a little sad. But he shouldn't be. Things are better this way.

"That's it," Joe announces at the end of Reflections. "Garrett?"

"Yes, sir?"

"Lead the family back."

Huh? Me?

"Is there a problem?" Joe asks.

"No, sir!" I jump to my feet. Leading the family is a job for a teen guard. This is a big step toward the upper levels.

"Hand in your markers and notebooks, everyone— let's go," I tell them.

The members of Dignity family start to get up. This is really good. Once I'm a Level Five, I'll be able to grow my hair longer and watch movies in the upper-level lounge.

The door opens, and a guy named Jason from Respect family comes in.

"What is it?" Joe asks.

"Mr. Z wants Garrett in his office, sir."

"Now?" Joe frowns. It's almost Shut Down, a strange time for Mr. Z to be asking to see anyone.

"Yes, sir. Right now."

Joe glances my way. Ever since the trouble I caused, there's a new rule that two staff members are supposed to accompany residents at all times. But I'll have to go with Jason alone.

"Can I trust you, Garrett?" Joe asks.

"Absolutely, sir." He doesn't have to worry about me doing anything wrong. Not after all I've been through.

"All right, you can go."

Jason and I leave the food hall. It's a clear winter night, and the icy air fills my lungs. The ground under our shoes is frozen. The grass crunches, the trees are bare, and there's a big, round, bright moon.

"Garrett!"

The woman's voice sounds so familiar, but for a moment I can't understand why. A figure is hurrying toward me in the dark, silhouetted by the outdoor lights. It's . . . my mother! She's wearing a red ski parka. Her hands are jammed in the pockets, and the ends of her blond hair peek out from under a fur hat. People are following her. There's my father in a heavy sweater and a down vest, and a man in a dark suit and topcoat, and another woman. Clouds of vapor escape their lips.

"Oh, honey!" My mother pulls me close and hugs

me hard. I can smell her perfume. "Are you all right?"

"Yes, ma'am."

She leans back and stares at me uncertainly. Her forehead is furrowed with concern. "Are you sure?"

"Yes, ma'am. Uh, what are you doing here, ma'am?"

She pulls me close and hugs me again. It feels a little strange because of the no-touch rule. Being so close to Level Five, I sure don't want to get in any trouble now. Meanwhile, her lips move close to my ear as she whispers, "You don't have to call me ma'am. I'm your mother. I'm here to take you out of this place. You can tell the truth, Garrett. I know what's been going on."

She backs away slightly but holds onto my shoulders. Now my father and the man in the topcoat and the other woman join us. Behind them is Mr. Z. I realize that the other woman is Rebecca. She takes my hand in hers.

"I found your parents," she says. "I told them how you saved our lives."

"We weren't sure whether to believe her," my father says. "But then we heard from a young woman in Canada. Someone named Sarah."

"Were you hit, or beaten, or injured at any time by a staff member?" the man in the topcoat asks.

I hesitate when Mr. Z catches my eye and clenches his jaw in warning.

"They said you were beaten," my father says. "Is that true?"

Mr. Z glares at me and shakes his head. My mother sees this.

"You can tell us the truth, Garrett," she pleads. "Don't pay any attention to that man. It doesn't matter now. We're taking you home. I promise you'll never see him again."

"Were you hit, or beaten, or kicked or injured at any time by a staff member?" the man in the topcoat asks again.

Mr. Z's eyes narrow into a furious glare. I know my mother said I'd never see him again, but I'm still afraid.

"Tell us the truth, Garrett," my father urges. "Did they hurt you?"

"I . . . I . . . Yes, sir, they did." I feel Mr. Z's eyes on me. "But—"

"But what?" my father asks.

"But . . . . I deserved it, sir."

AFTERWORD

A secret prison system for teenagers exists in the United States. Many have never heard of it, and even among those who have, few understand what it really is or how it works. You do not have to be found guilty of a crime to be placed in one of these prisons, also known as boot camps. You do not even have to be accused of committing a crime. All you have to do is be under the age of eighteen.

It is impossible to know how many boot camps exist. Estimates put the number between one hundred and two hundred, and the number of teens in them between four thousand and ten thousand. Most boot camps avoid publicity, preferring instead to advertise their services privately and by word of mouth. In addition a number of boot camps have been set up outside United States borders—especially in Central America and the Caribbean, but also as far away as Thailand and the Philippines—to avoid American regulations against the mistreatment of teenage detainees.

Mistreatment of teens in boot camps is well documented. On a daily basis teens in these camps are forced to endure the intense physical demands of prolonged exercise, runs, drills, and outdoor hikes in extreme heat or cold. Food is often close to inedible, and medical care is scant. In the past twenty years close to forty young people between the ages of thirteen and seventeen have died in these facilities, often as a result of physical abuse, malnourishment, and neglect.

There are different types of boot camps. Some are state-run; others are privately operated. Some have a religious orientation. All have the following in common:

1) The mission of accepting "defiant," "unruly," "out-of-control" teens and the promise of returning a child who is "respectful," "polite," and "obedient."

2) Rigorous and often torturous physical, emotional, and psychological agendas aimed at "reprogramming" young residents.

3) Extremely tight security—surveillance cameras, motion detectors, walls topped with broken glass, and razor-wire fences—designed to insure that no one escapes.

Demand for the services of these camps is high, allowing some facilities, which dub themselves "specialty schools" and "behavior modification programs," to charge up to forty thousand dollars a year. The average stay is one to three years.

While "defiant" teens make up the bulk of the population in these programs, boot camps are wide-reaching in whom they will accept, including teens described as "depressed," "failing in school," "pregnant," "suffering from attention deficit disorder or hyperactivity," "truant," "promiscuous," "having feelings of despair," "suffering emotional problems," or "lacking motivation."

In at least one case, a seventeen-year-old girl was sent to a well-known boot camp because of an "unsuitable choice of boyfriend."

While many teenagers will at times feel depressed or unmotivated or have emotional problems, they have no legal rights or recourse should their parents decide to send them away. It is perfectly legal for parents to hire professional kidnappers, who prefer to be called "transporters," to abduct their children and deliver them to the desired facility.

Once in a boot camp, teens are cut off from the outside world. They are not allowed to communicate with anyone except their parents, who are warned in advance that complaints of physical abuse and maltreatment are lies—attempts by their child to "manipulate" them in order to be taken out of the boot camp. All forms of news and current entertainment are forbidden in order to reinforce the impression that the world inside the boot camp is the only thing that matters.

At the age of eighteen, teens are legally considered adults and therefore allowed to leave the facility if they choose. But teens under the age of eighteen have no choice. Should parents decide for any reason that they've had enough of a child, they can sentence him or her to boot camp. And the child is helpless to stop them.

REFERENCE LIST

The information for this book came from many sources. While the books and articles I drew on for research were too numerous to mention, below is a list of some of the more important ones:

1) Capeloto, Alex. "Inside the Macomb County Youth Home," *Detroit Free Press*, September, 2003.
2) Cohen, Adam. "Is This a Camp or a Jail?" *Time* magazine, January 26, 1998.
3) Collier, Lorna. "The Last Resort," *Chicago Tribune*, May 27, 2001.
4) Halbfinger, David. "Care of Juvenile Offenders in Mississippi is Faulted", *New York Times*, Sept 1, 2003.
5) Hargrove, Mary. "Beat Him Up and Do Him Good. Don't Leave Any Marks," *Arkansas Democrat-Gazette*, June 1998.
6) Janofsky, Michael. "Accounts Put Darker Cloud Over Camp," *New York Times*, July 4, 2001.
7) Kent, Stephen A., and Hall, Deana. *Brainwashing and Re-Indoctrination Programs in the Children of God/The Family*, University of Alberta, abstract published in *Cultic Studies Journal*, Volume 17 (2000): 56-78.
8) Keri J. "Surviving Survival Camp" www.nospank.net
9) Krajicek, David. "Time To Stick a Fork in America's Correctional Boot Camp Boondoggle," MSNBC, December 23, 1999.

10) Labi, Nadya. "Want Your Kid to Disappear?" transcript from *Leonard Lopate Show*, WNYC, July 1, 2004.

11) Leonard, Andrew. "Schools of Hard Knocks" *Salon*, February 23, 1998.

12) Parks, Alexia. *An American Gulag*, The Education Exchange, Eldorado Springs, CO, 2000.

13) Riak, Jordan. "Deadly Restraint" www.nospank. net, January, 2003.

14) Selcraig, Bruce. "Camp Fear" *Mother Jones Magazine*, December, 2000.

15) Smith, Christopher. "Tough Love Proves Too Tough: The Short Life and Hard Death of a Teenager", *High Country News*, Paonia, CO, June 10, 1996.

16) Vosepka, Rich. "Texas Teenager Dies in Utah Wilderness Program", Associated Press, July 16, 2002.

17) Weiner, Tim. "Parents Divided Over Jamaica Disciplinary Academy," *New York Times*, June 17, 2003.

18) "Boot Camps for Teens," promotional materials.

19) *The Last Resort, The London Observer Magazine*, June 29, 2003.

20) "When Discipline Turns Fatal," www.nospank.net.

21) *The World Wide Association of Specialty Programs and Schools*, promotional pamphlet.

About the Author

TODD STRASSER has written many award-winning novels for teenagers, including *Can't Get There from Here*; *Give a Boy a Gun*; and *How I Created My Perfect Prom Date*, which became the motion picture *Drive Me Crazy*. He lives in a suburb of New York City. Visit Todd at www.toddstrasser.com.

Want to read more riveting fiction
by Todd Strasser?
Don't miss **Give a Boy a Gun**.

Part of Gary Searle's
Suicide Note

Dear Mom,

By the time you read this, I'll
be gone. I just want you to know that
there's nothing you could have done
to stop this. I know you always tried
your best for me, and if anyone doubts
you, just show them this letter.

I don't know if I can really explain
why I did this. I guess it's because I
know that I'll never be happy. I know
that every day of my life will hurt
and be a lot more bad than good. It's
entirely a matter of, What's the point
of living?

Introduction

Around 10 P.M. on Friday, February 27, Gary Searle died in the gymnasium at Middletown High School. After the bullet smashed through the left side of his skull and tore into his brain, he probably lived for ten to fifteen seconds.

The brain is a fragile organ suspended in a liquid environment. Not only does a bullet destroy whatever brain tissue is in its path, but the shock waves from the impact severely jar the entire organ, ripping apart millions of delicate structures and connections. In the seconds that follow, the brain swells with blood and other fluids. The parts of the brain that control breathing and heartbeat stop. One doctor described it to me as "an earthquake in the head."

At the moment of Gary's death I was in the library at the state university, where I was a sophomore studying journalism. As soon as I heard the news, I went home to Middletown, determined not to leave until I understood what had happened there.

Returning to Middletown was like stepping into a thick fog of bewilderment, fury, agony, and despair. For weeks I staggered through it, searching out other lost, wandering souls. Some were willing to talk to me. Others spoke because they felt a need to defend themselves even though no one had pointed an accusing finger at them. Some even sought me out because they *wanted* to talk. As if speaking about it was a way of trying to figure it out, of beginning the long, painful process of grieving and moving ahead.

Some refused to speak because it must have been too painful. For others, I suspect it was because they had learned something about themselves that they were still struggling to accept—or to conceal.

I spoke to everyone who would speak to me. In addition I studied everything I could find on the many similar incidents that have occurred in other schools around our country in the past thirty years.

The story you are about to read is really two stories. One is about what happened here in Middletown. The other is the broader tale of what is happening all around our country—in a world of schools and guns and violence that has forever changed the place I once called home. The quotes and facts from other incidents are in a different-style print. What happened in Middletown is in plain print.

This, then, is the story of what I learned. It is told in many voices, in words far more eloquent and raw than any I could have thought of on my own. It is a story of heartbreak and fear and regret. But mostly it is a warning. Violence comes in many forms—guns, fists, and words of hate and contempt. Unless we change the way we treat others in school and out, there will only be more—and more horrible—tragedies.

LOOKING FOR THE PERFECT BEACH READ?